I0589758

CYNTHIA HICKEY

TO BREATHE AGAIN
A Highland Springs suspense novel, Book 3
By Cynthia Hickey

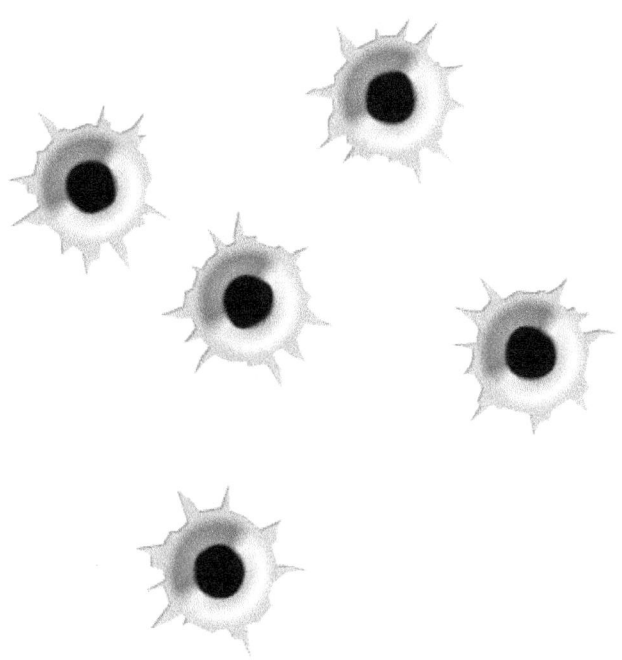

ISBN-13: 978-1-0881-4665-1

DEDICATION

To all those eagerly waiting for another Sheriff Camenetti story.

Prologue

The Reverend Donald Bishop smiled across the table at his family. He was richer than he'd ever dreamed, and his followers grew every day. His oldest, and only son, sat at his right hand. Together, they ruled Highland Mountain, the imposing structure that overlooked the town of Highland Springs. It was time to grow his family even further, and their new town was ripe for the taking.

He'd followed the career of Rachel Smith with much interest and taken note of how easy it was for her to take the children. Of course, he'd helped her out a time or two when a child didn't meet his criteria, and gained wealth in the process.

He wasn't worried about the sheriff and her deputies. Not at all. Six months had passed, and the town had let down its guard. Besides, it wasn't babies he was interested in anymore. Young women and strong men were what he needed.

Chapter One

Sharlene Camenetti, Sheriff of Highland Springs, smiled at her son, Robby, and at his biological mother, Mira, who despite having just turned eighteen, wanted to stay with Shar. At the stove, Candy, Shar's sister, poured pancake batter into a sizzling skillet. Life had settled down into a pleasant routine.

"I, for one, am more than pleased that things are once again boring in this town." Candy turned down the flame on the burner.

"Not me," Mira said, crossing her arms. "I'm bored silly."

"Even with school?" Shar shook her head. She couldn't remember the last time she was bored, low crime or not. After the online murders Lars Townsend had perpetrated and the baby snatching Rachel Smith had been guilty of, she yearned for near boredom.

"Tell me again why you're forcing me to go to school?" Mira frowned. "It's so hard, and I'm too far behind."

"You'll catch up. You're smart." Shar winked and

wiped the baby food from Robby's chin. She worried every time Mira walked out the door that the girl would head back to her old ways of boys, drugs, and violence.

Shar put Robby into his carrier, shouldered her holster, and headed to her jeep. A short time later, she deposited her son into the capable hands of the workers at the daycare, newly built after the explosion six months earlier. She grinned and kissed his forehead. Now, it was time for coffee.

She parked in front of the coffee shop and waited while a solidly built middle-aged man, a tiny sparrow of a woman, and five blond girls shuffled past. If not for the man's expensive suit and the lack of a head covering on the women, she would have thought them Mennonite. The only one with his head not bowed was the man. Shar hadn't seen them before.

Pushing open her door, she followed them into the drugstore. "Good morning. I'm Sheriff Camenetti. Welcome to Highland Springs." She thrust out her hand.

The man grinned a too-white, too-wide smile and clasped her hand in a strong shake. "Reverend Donald Bishop of the Church of Superior Essence. My family and I recently bought land up on the mountain. We're here to save the lost while there is still time."

The church of what? She kept a smile on her face, welcomed them again to her town, and headed for coffee. Why would a church of that type be setting up shop in America's Bible Belt? She shrugged and pushed open the coffee shop door.

"The usual?" Jen, the barista, glanced in her direction from her position behind the register.

"Yep. Four of the usual." She leaned against the

counter and watched the reverend and his family head back the way they'd come. "Do you know anything about that group?"

"Nope." Jen shrugged. "I've seen them walking around a time or two, but they haven't come in."

Shar smiled. "They're here to save the world." She collected the coffee, set the carrier carefully on the front passenger seat and drove to the sheriff's office.

Everis glanced up from his desk. "Good morning, beautiful."

"Good morning, handsome. Bored yet?" After discovering he had a son, and then taking custody of the three-year-old, Everis had stepped down from his position with the Arkansas Federal Bureau of Investigations and took the job as Shar's third deputy and all around right-hand man.

"Not at all. Brian keeps me busy. I come to work to relax." He grinned and took the drink she offered. "Mayfield and Pinson are out."

She set the carrier on the desk and sat down. While her computer booted up, she flipped through the messages on her desk. A couple of vandalisms, and a man violating a restraining order by urinating on his ex-wife's lawn. She sighed. "Are Mayfield and Pinson taking care of these?"

"Yep."

Good. Shar loved her job as sheriff, but sometimes the nitty-gritty stuff exhausted her. She sipped her coffee and studied the profile of the man she loved. Oh, she hadn't said the words yet, nor had he, but the feeling was there. Everis had risked his life multiple times to save Shar. She couldn't think of a better person to have by her side.

Rachel number three, as she had been called for the last two years, cupped her hands under her pregnant belly and continued her mad stumbling dash through the thick woods. She could barely remember her real name of Amy. She had to get away. If her child was a boy, he'd take it away from her. He'd done so in the past. She would no longer be one of his wives, fit for nothing more than to carry his offspring.

Why had she believed in his lies, his promises? She put out a hand and braced herself against a tree to catch her breath. Hounds brayed in the distance. They were coming.

She pressed on. A cliff over a river stopped her flight.

The braying grew closer.

She stared at the water below her. Could she chance it? Yes. Better to jump than go back to him.

"No, Rachel!"

She glanced back. He sprinted toward her. Taking a deep breath, she squeezed her eyes shut and jumped.

Imbecile! Foolish girl. He stared into the river and watched her bob like a cork. Couldn't she see her importance in the coming new world? Women with good bloodlines and the breeding ability were priceless. Especially the blond, blue-eyed ones.

He cursed and headed back to the others. Toward men who were nothing more than workers. Until they proved their worth, they weren't allowed to father any children. The men struggling with the dog leashes had a very long way to go before that happened.

"Find her," he ordered, shoving past them. "Dead or

alive, I want her brought back." His father would be very displeased at Rachel's escape and would punish him.

*
*
*

Everis returned Shar's heated stare. He knew from experience how her cheeks turned pink before she ducked her head. Yep. There she went. He won the staring contest every time.

Loud voices signaled the return of the other two deputies. Both made a beeline for the coffee on Shar's desk.

"It's cold." Pinson frowned.

"It wasn't when I arrived." Shar trained her ice-blue glare on him. "Fill me in."

"The two boys painting male body parts on park signs are waiting for you in the conference room. The man who urinated on his ex-wife's rose bushes is in the holding cell." Pinson glanced at Mayfield. "Did I forget anything?"

"That about covers it. Give me your drink and I'll nuke it."

Pinson handed over his coffee. "Are you going to put the fear of God in those twerps or do you want me to?"

Shar shook her head. "Everis and I will."

Everis loved to watch Shar interact with her people. The town belonged to her. She loved the citizens, treated them fairly, and they loved her. Her sheriff mask slipped into place as she got to her feet and strode from the room. With a grin, Everis followed.

"Boys." Shar placed a notepad squarely in front of a chair and took her seat. "Names."

"You know who we are."

"Yes, I do, but I need them stated for the record." She nodded for Everis to turn on the recorder.

"Mason Monroe and Bobby Miller."

Shar folded her hands on top of the notepad and fixed a stare on Mason. "Do I even need to ask who the ringleader was?"

"No." He slouched in his seat. "There's nothing to do in this town."

"You're supposed to be in school. That's something to do. Have you considered a job in the afternoons?" Everis perched on the corner of the table. "I hear the park ranger is looking for help."

Shar smiled. "That's a great idea. After you work for free paying off the damage from your artwork."

"You can't force us to work." Mason cut a sideways glance at Bobby.

"Not on a permanent basis, no. But," she leaned across the table, "I can strongly suggest it. Look, boys. I believe in the baseball rule. Three strikes and you're out. This is your third strike. Next time, I'll take you to court and have you thrown in juvie. Got it?"

Faces pale, they nodded.

"Good. Now find something constructive to do until this weekend. You'll work every weekend for twelve weeks. Have a good day." She marched from the conference room.

"I guess that leaves calling your parents up to me," Everis said.

"Do you have to?" Bobby asked.

"Yep. Look, boys. Nobody is going to change things but you. Your file in this office is two-inches thick. You won't like juvie, I guarantee it." He pushed the phone on one end of the table to the center. "I think

I'll let you call your parents."

"Aw, man." Mason grabbed the receiver and dialed. "Can you pick me up…at the sheriff's office…vandalism."

Everis didn't think it possible, but the boy paled even further. He almost felt sorry for him. "Your turn, Bobby."

When they'd both finished calling, Everis left, closing the conference room door behind him. They weren't going anywhere until their parents arrived. Before returning to the office, he stopped by Amber's reception desk. "Those boys don't leave with anyone but their own parents."

"Got it." She nodded, her sculpted nails flying over the keyboard. "Parents."

Everis chuckled. Amber looked like she charged on the street corner, but a sharp mind existed under all that hair and a hard worker under the tight, flashy clothes. Shar had done well getting this girl off the streets.

The phone rang as he headed back to the office. Amber answered with a "howdy, Sheriff's office."

Shaking his head, Everis grabbed a mug from the lounge and filled it with black coffee. He wasn't kidding when he said he needed to come to work to get some rest. He moved back to his desk.

Amber rushed into the room. "Got a person in the river."

Chapter Two

"Alive?" Shar shot a glance over her shoulder.

Amber shrugged. "They didn't say. I'll send directions to your cell phone."

Shar's phone pinged with a text message as she climbed into the driver's seat of her jeep. She tossed the phone to Everis. "Give directions, please."

"Turn right at the big rock? Seriously, people get places like this?"

She laughed. "Some of the side roads out here don't have official names." She veered right where a boulder jutted out of the ground.

"Left at the tree that was struck by lightning."

She followed the instructions, smiling at the incredulous look on his face, and pulled behind a pair of four-wheelers. Hopping out, she asked Everis to call Mayfield and Pinson to come secure the scene, then headed for the edge of the water where four young people huddled together.

One of the boys stepped forward. "I pulled her from

the water and performed CPR. She's alive."

Surprised, Shar thanked him. "You may have saved her life." She knelt next to a pretty blonde, very pregnant, young girl around the age of eighteen or nineteen. The plain, cotton nightgown she wore left little to the imagination in its soaked state. Shar removed her jacket and draped it over the girl to provide a bit of modesty.

"Do you know her?" she asked the boy.

"No. None of us do. She was halfway out of the water when we drove up. I pulled her out of those dead branches." He motioned to a pile of wood in the water.

"I've called for an ambulance." Everis stood over her shoulder.

Shar felt for a pulse and watched the slow rise and fall of the girl's chest. "I hope they hurry. She's alive, but barely." Planting her hands on her thighs, she pushed to her feet. "No identification. She's wearing nothing but a nightgown. My guess is she's about eight months pregnant."

"No one has reported her missing. At least not around here." He turned as the ambulance wailed to a stop behind the jeep. "Do you want me to get the statements while you take care of her?"

Shar nodded. She'd had too much interaction with pregnant teens in the last year. Knowing how frightened most of them were, well, she didn't want to leave the unknown girl alone. Hopefully, they would be able to find her family.

She stepped back as the paramedics worked on her. Not once did the girl regain consciousness. A lump the size of an egg poked through bangs plastered to her forehead. Shar wasn't a doctor, but she'd bet the poor thing had a concussion. She transferred her attention to the swift-moving river.

The girl could have fallen in miles upriver. But why would she be out in her nightgown? It didn't compute. Shar moved to the edge of the water and peered into the branches Jane Doe had been pulled from. Nothing. No jewelry, no purse, no shoes. Not a single thing that might tell her who the girl was. Standing as close to the water as she could without getting her shoes wet, she stared upriver.

Sheer rock walls rose on each side. A cliff jutted out right before the river bend. The shape of a man stood on the edge. He seemed to glance her way, then melted into the trees.

Shar's gut told her the girl hadn't fallen willingly. She pivoted and headed for her jeep as the deputies approached. "Everis, tell those kids to give their statements at the station. Mayfield, Pinson, secure the scene. Everis and I are taking a ride."

It took almost an hour to find a bridge to cross, then several wrong stops before she found the cliff in question. She knew this because she could see her deputies working down river. Shar shoved open her door.

"Are you going to tell me what's going on, or should I take a guess?" Everis matched her stride to the cliff's edge.

"I saw a man standing here. When he saw me watching, he moved back out of sight." She scanned the ground.

"You think he pushed our girl?"

"I don't know." Paw prints mingled with shoe prints. Bare feet made a beeline for the edge. Booted prints followed the same trail. "She was running. See how far apart her prints are?"

"Chased by dogs?"

"And people." Shar approached the edge. "Her prints and one other set stop here." A chill ran down her spine. "Do you think she jumped to get away from whoever was following her?"

"It's a possibility we can't ignore."

Shar turned at the sound of a car engine revving. Where? She whirled, trying to pinpoint the sound. It faded away.

*
* *

"I'm sorry." Everis rested a hand on her shoulder. He wanted to kiss the disappointment from her face.

She pulled away. "Don't you dare promise me we'll get to the bottom of this."

"Okay." But they would. They always caught their man, or woman.

"I know what you're thinking." Shar stormed toward the jeep and pulled crime scene tape from the back. "We do catch our guy, but often at great expense." She handed one end of the tape to him and moved to a tree opposite. Soon, they'd made a large box cordoning off what looked to be a popular sightseeing spot. Shar pulled her cell phone from her pocket and started snapping photos.

Everis did the same. Other than foot and paw prints, the area revealed no clues. "Let's head to the hospital and see if they've discovered anything about our Jane Doe."

"Can't do anything else here." She cast another glance toward the cliff, then climbed into her jeep.

By the time they arrived at the hospital, Jane Doe

had been assigned a room. A Doctor Kuchra put her file into a holder on the wall and greeted them. "She hasn't woken up yet. Quite a bang on the head. The baby seems to be doing fine. We've put the mother into a medical coma for a day or two to make sure her vitals stay strong."

"Any idea who she is?" Shar stared at the girl in the bed.

"Nope. The newspaper is going to post her picture inside. Maybe someone will come forth." He shook his head. "Sad." He left them alone.

"Good afternoon, Sheriff." A large man entered the room. His gaze settled on Everis.

"Everis, this is Reverend Donald Bishop," Shar said, not moving from the side of the bed.

"Nice to meet you, sir. Do you know this girl?"

"No, but I was visiting a parishioner of mine and heard of her plight. I thought I'd come pray with her family."

"We haven't located them."

"Tragic." His smile looked forced as he bent over the girl in the bed. "How is she?"

"Coma." Something about the man didn't sit right with Everis. His booming voice, overly friendly expression, and the way his eyes narrowed when he stared down at Jane Doe seemed off.

"We will add her to our prayer list." He handed Everis a business card. "If you'd like." He flashed a big grin at Shar and left.

"He didn't invite me to church when I met him." Shar sat in the salmon chair next to the bed.

"Church of Superior Essence? What in the hell is that?"

"No idea. Maybe we can have Pinson check it out."

"If he gets invited." Everis chuckled, then peered out the door and down the hall.

The reverend glanced back as he entered the elevator. The smile no longer filled his face. Instead, his expression had hardened to granite. Everis watched until the doors closed.

"What is it?" Shar asked.

Everis faced her. "Something weird about that man." He'd learned a long time ago to trust his instincts. He glanced at the card in his hand. "Maybe I'll be attending church on Sunday. Want to go?"

She sighed and stood. "I wasn't invited. Tell me how it goes."

"You seem to be taking it personal."

"No, it isn't about the reverend." She met his gaze. "This town is full of teenage mothers. I know this region isn't as educated as most—young people get bored—but I'd really like to find a way to help."

"The fact you care as much as you do is a great help to the people of this town." He grasped her hand and gave a gentle squeeze. "Come on. Let's find out who Jane Doe is. We can discuss things over lunch. Burger?"

"With bacon and mushrooms."

Shar drove them to an outside diner and chose a table under a blue-and-white striped umbrella. "This place is closed during winter or bad weather, but they serve the best burgers."

Everis sat across from her and studied the menu under the table top glass. "Nothing but burgers and fries. Perfect." He'd found that places that focused on one specialty item were definitely worth trying.

"Mason?" Shar looked up as the town's busiest delinquent approached to take their orders.

"My dad agreed with you and made me get a job. Since I chose to ditch school, he made me use that time to find one. I work every afternoon once school lets out. Thanks a lot." He shrugged. "I kind of like the fact I'll be making my own money and spending it how I want."

She flashed a grin. "I'm proud of you. I'll take the number three basket with a large diet Coke."

"The same." Everis leaned back in his chair. "See? You helped that boy simply by being consistent in the way you treat him. You've been voted into your second term as sheriff. This town loves and needs you."

"You could do this job."

He shook his head. "No, I couldn't always keep my composure like you do. I'm not able to put on a mask and take it off at the end of the day."

"You need to give yourself more credit." She met his gaze. "You're one of the most wonderful people I've ever met."

"Are you finally admitting that you're falling for me." He grinned.

"Never." Her cheeks turned a bright shade of pink. With her dark hair, almost grey eyes, and pale skin, there was no way she could ever hide a blush.

"Liar." He glanced up to see Reverend Bishop and a pack of women head to the library.

"Yesterday, they went to the drugstore," Shar said, following his gaze.

"Probably inviting people to church."

"The women look kind of sad, don't you think?"

"That man is a commanding presence. I'm sure they're used to fading into the background."

The crack of the whip sent a blast of pain across his back. Ten lashes, as ordered by his father for losing Rachel. He hissed as another lash ripped his skin. By the time the administrator finished, blood trickled down his back and sweat beaded his brow.

"Discipline," his father said from his seat in the dark corner of the room. "Without it, our new world will fall. Not only must we discipline our followers, but our family. You need to find another wife. We cannot populate without them."

"I will. I'll head to Alabama tomorrow. I'll be back within the month with a bride." He took his shirt from the back of a nearby chair and gingerly slid his arms into the sleeves. "Maybe more than one."

"Blond, blue-eyed, and of breeding age."

"Yes, Father. I know."

"Very well." His father stood. "Have your wives tend to your back. We need to figure out what we're going to do with the one in the hospital."

He jerked. "Will she survive?"

"It's unclear. It appears as if they are trying to save the infant. Unfortunately, we cannot step forward and lay claim, so it's a waste."

"Not if it's a dark-haired boy." One less thing for him to get rid of. "We do need more men fathering children."

His father grinned. "I have a new plan in mind, and someone very motivated to help me succeed with that plan. Perhaps we aren't completely correct by insisting on only blond and blue eyes. I felt a powerful strength in a dark-haired man. After all, we don't know what Adam and Eve looked like, do we? No more getting rid of the children.   With Rachel Smith dead, we have no one else we can trust anyway. Time is drawing to an end. We need every worthy person we can find."

CYNTHIA HICKEY

Chapter Three

The man stood on the outskirts of the high school ground. He'd found the girls he thought would suit the one he wanted to impress. Right now, he gained wealth from helping the leader of the new world. Soon, he'd be a member and sit at the man's right hand.

Now that they no longer needed to look like clones, opportunity abounded. The two brunettes and the redhead were perfect.

He glanced at an African American girl. She'd proven she could bear children. Maybe it wouldn't hurt to ask whether his leader wanted to expand into other ethnic groups. Diversity could continue in the new world, better than ever with new laws in place.

As the girls passed, he pulled his cap low over his eyes and turned, bending over the fire hydrant and pretended to inspect it. When they'd moved ahead of him, he followed, careful to stay far enough back as to not attract attention.

One of the brunettes veered off from the others and mounted the steps of a red brick house. She turned to wave, her gaze sweeping over him before she entered the house. The other two girls waved back and continued on their way.

Wonderful. They would pass right by the best place for him to abduct them.

He'd parked his blue panel van a few yards down a tree-shaded street, and just as he'd hoped, the girls headed in that direction. He would have to act fast before they got within sight of the cluster of houses at the top of the hill.

Pulling a Taser from inside his light jacket, he darted forward. He pressed the tip to the closest girl, catching her as she fell. "Do not scream," he told the other, "or I will kill you. Do you understand?"

She nodded, tears filling her eyes.

"Get in the van." He shoved the girl in his arms inside, gagged both of them, then bound the girls' hands with zip ties and climbed into the driver's seat. "It's a whole new world, girls!"

He drove to the compound, sticking to back roads, and parked behind the building where he knew the reverend doled out punishment to his followers. He opened the back of the van. "Do not make a sound."

He dragged the girls from the van and prodded them into the building where the reverend waited. "Two fine young women for you."

"Very nice." The reverend walked a slow circle around them. "Once they're trained and submissive, they will do very nicely indeed." He snapped his fingers. Two men stepped forward, each taking one of the girls by the arms and leading them through a side door.

"Your compensation will be in your account by the

end of the day."

"Are you interested in young girls with darker skin?"

The reverend rubbed his chin. "Why limit ourselves? You know what I'm looking for. If you are to become one of my future elders, I need to be able to trust your judgment."

* * *

"Frantic mother on line two," Amber shouted on her way to the staff lounge. "Daughter didn't come home from school."

"Got it." Shar grabbed the receiver to her desk phone. "Sheriff Camenetti, how may I help you?"

"This is Laura Helms. My daughter Lauren didn't come home from school. Neither did her best friend, Megan Tims."

Shar glanced at the wall clock. School let out an hour ago. "They're probably hanging out with their friends. Have you called all of them?"

"Yes. I called Sara Horn. She said they headed home." The woman's voice cracked. "When I told her they didn't arrive here, she said she thought a man might have been following them."

Shar jotted down all the names. "Call Sara and tell her I'll be there in ten minutes." She hung up the phone and grabbed the keys to her jeep.

Everis fell into step beside her on the way across the parking lot. She explained where she was headed and why.

"I'll tag along if you don't mind."

"Of course, I don't mind." In fact, she'd like him to accompany her everywhere always. She never thought she'd find a man who could hold her heart in his hands and cause her to second-guess the priority she placed on her career. Now, here was Everis, she had a son, and she was helping a former juvenile teen get her life together. Her life had become fuller than she'd ever imagined.

Sara Horn opened the door to her house before Shar could lift her hand to knock. "Did that man take them? Are they kidnapped?"

"We'll need to investigate before coming to that conclusion." Shar smiled. "May we come in?"

"Oh, yeah. My parents aren't here."

"We'll need to speak to one of them and obtain permission to question you." Shar glanced around the small foyer. A dining room, a den, and what looked like a coat closet branched off.

"I'll call my mom. Go ahead and sit in the living room." She pressed buttons on her cell phone and followed them into the room. "Mom, the sheriff is here. No, I'm not in trouble. Lauren and Megan are missing, and they want to ask me some questions. Will you tell the sheriff it's okay?" She handed the phone to Shar.

"Ma'am, do we have your permission to ask Sara some questions?"

"Of course. I hope everything is okay. Megan has a tendency to be a bit on the wild side. They're probably smoking at the lake."

"Something we will consider. Thank you." Shar texted Mayfield and asked him to check the lake and surrounding area for the two girls. "Now, what's this about a man?"

Sara plopped onto a tan sofa. "We left school just like always. This man was fixing the fire hydrant. I saw him again when I arrived at my house. There aren't any fire hydrants in my yard."

Shar made a mental note to check up on anyone working on fire hydrants around town. "Can you describe this man?"

"Not really. He wore a blue jacket, a dark blue baseball cap, and jeans. I couldn't see his face."

"Can you tell us how old, his height, weight, anything more?"

She shook her head.

"How do Lauren and Megan usually walk home? What direction?"

"They go to the end of my street, turn right, then turn onto that road with all the trees."

"Thank you, Sara." Shar leaned forward, balancing her elbows on her knees and focused on the girl's face. "I'd like you to continue trying to get a hold of your friends. Can you do that?"

"I won't stop." She swiped the back of her hand across her eyes. "Ever."

"What do you think?" Shar asked once she and Everis stepped outside. "Missing or partying?"

He shrugged. "I can't really make a guess without knowing the girls, but if they were partying, Sara wouldn't be as upset. Unless she's a really good actress."

"Hmm." She called Mayfield. "Anything?"

"Nope. Not a single teenager in sight. My guess is they'll converge on the lake tomorrow night. Friday, you know?"

"Yeah. Thanks." She hung up. "Not at the lake." She glanced in the direction the girls should have gone. "We might as well trace their steps."

They turned left. Everis scanned the ground and surrounding area, taking note of a gum wrapper and a cigarette butt. There seemed to be some scuff marks, but it was unclear if someone struggling caused them. Knowing they probably weren't related to the girls' possible disappearance, he used a tissue from his pocket to pick up the wrapper and the cigarette butt.

Stopping at the end of the tree-lined road, he stared at a dilapidated chicken house. "These types of buildings give me the creeps."

"Me, too." Shar climbed through the barbed wire of the fence surrounding the pasture and led the way to the rundown building. "Hello? This is the sheriff. Anyone inside?"

Everis used his shoulder to push open the sagging door. It was obvious at first glance that no one had been inside for quite some time. The building now contained only bales of hay for the cattle milling in the pasture.

Moving back to the road, they continued walking, Shar on one side, Everis the other. "Here." He squatted next to a set of fresh tire tracks. "Not saying the girls went away in this vehicle, but it's worth a look." He snapped a photo of the tracks with his cell phone. "Want to talk to the parents up the hill?"

"Definitely."

They hiked up the hill and rang the bell of the home of Lauren Helms. A woman with red-rimmed eyes and worry lines greeted them. "Thank God." She stepped back and ushered them inside. "Did you find my daughter?"

"No, ma'am," Shar said. "We're actively searching for them."

The woman fell into a chair. "I've called every one

of their friends. No one has seen them since seventh period."

"I know this is difficult," Everis said, "but did you and your daughter have a fight recently?"

"Lauren did not run away. She's graduating with honors. Why throw that away?" She shook her head. "Something happened to them."

"Do you have a recent photo of your daughter?"

She jumped up. "I have one with both her and Megan in it." She rushed away, returning with a senior picture and a photograph with the three girls. In it a pretty blonde and laughing brunette with their arms draped around each other, posed for a selfie.

Neither of them looked like an unhappy teen. Everis held out his hand. "May we have this?"

She nodded. "I've another copy." She gripped his hand. "Please, find my daughter."

He wanted to promise her, same as he always promised Shar when doubts and fears surfaced, but truth be told, a lot of young women who disappeared were never seen again. "We will do everything in our power."

He promised to work hard, never stop looking until the girls were home, and to pray.

Chapter Four

Nothing. None of the phone calls or door-to-door questioning revealed a single clue as to where the missing girls might be. Shar sighed and rubbed her eyes. "Any hits on their cell phones?"

"Nope." Everis handed her a cup of coffee. "Mayfield and Pinson are continuing the search down every street in town, but with the late hour, folks don't want to answer the door."

"They might not be in town. Thanks." She took the offered cup. "One of the mothers found her daughter's social media password and called me. I'm getting ready to go online now." She angled the monitor so Everis could see.

She typed in the password and pulled up Megan Tims' profile. "In a relationship. Why didn't her mother mention a boyfriend?"

"Is there a name?"

"Scott."

"I'll call Sara. See whether we can get a last name." He moved to his desk.

Shar continued to browse Megan's page and found absolutely nothing to warrant the girl taking off. A bad feeling about the teens' disappearance descended on her. The more she searched, the more convinced she became that the girls may have been abducted.

"Got two. Scott Milroy and Scott Baker. Let's make a late-night visit to a couple of boys." Everis held the door open.

"Maybe we'll get lucky and the girls are hanging with a boy their parents don't approve of."

He laughed. "I bet you never did."

"Not really," she said, smiling, "but Candy did plenty of times. Said the punishment was always worth the fun beforehand."

His grin widened. "I always found that to be true. Let's find these girls and take some time to be naughty ourselves."

Her face heated. "Behave and focus."

The man flirted incessantly, continuously leaving her flustered, and she loved every minute of it. Since he thought only of the job once they sat at their desks or hit the streets, she allowed herself the luxury of a few moments of feeling desirable when he was in a playful mood. Something she rarely felt, wearing a tan uniform with her hair shoved into a ponytail.

The first Scott they visited stepped onto the front porch to meet them. "My parents are sleeping. If this is about the party at the lake this weekend—"

Shar slipped her sheriff mask into place to fight back the urge to smile. "It isn't, but thank you for the heads-up. I'm sure there won't be any underage drinking."

"No, ma'am."

Everis cleared his throat. "Do you know Megan Tims or Lauren Helms?"

"They're only the hottest girls in the senior class. Well, two of the five hottest." He flashed a grin. Sara is hot, so is Mira. Then, there's that redhead…"

"My Mira?"

"Sassy, that one."

"That's enough." Shar shook her head. "Megan and Lauren didn't arrive home after school. Any idea where they might be?"

"Megan's boyfriend's house?"

"Who is?"

"Scott McIlroy."

"Thank you." Shar stared at the young man until his gaze locked with hers. "I'm serious about the party, Scott. No drinking, no drugs, no sex."

"No fun," he mumbled.

"Have a good evening." Shar turned and headed back to her jeep.

"You know they'll just change the location of the party, right?" Everis slid into the passenger seat.

"I know." She laughed. "But they'll be looking over their shoulders the whole time. Might help keep things from escalating out of control."

"We can always hope."

Less than five minutes later, they sat in the McIlroy family's living room across from Scott and his parents. "I haven't seen Megan since lunch," Scott said, hanging his hands between his knees. "We don't have any afternoon classes together."

"Would she have taken off?" Shar pierced the boy with her stare.

"Like run away?" He shook his head. "No, Megan has dreams. College, nursing school, stuff like that."

"Were you a part of those dreams?"

"Wait a minute, sheriff." Mr. McIlroy crossed his arms. "Are you insinuating that my son might have something to do with these girls' disappearance?"

"We aren't insinuating anything, sir, but we aren't going to refrain from questioning one of the people who knows the girls best." She turned back to Scott. "Answer my question, please?"

"I'm a part of her dreams, at least through college." He shrugged. "Anything can happen though, right?"

Just like a disappearance. Scott McIlroy just became their primary person of interest, mainly because they didn't have anyone else.

Shar handed Mr. McIlroy a business card. "Please call me if you think of anything that will help us find these girls."

Mrs. McIlroy stood. "I'll see you to the door, and we'll be praying for their safe return."

"Thank you." Shar paused on the porch steps and faced Everis. "What do you think?"

"It doesn't make sense that he would get rid of a girlfriend when there wasn't any animosity."

"I agree." Which left them back at zero.

She stepped off the porch and headed for the jeep. Halfway there, she pivoted to glance up at a second-story window. Scott stared down at them, then let the curtains fall into place.

*　*　*

"We've come to help search for the girls." Reverend Bishop approached Everis the next morning in the parking lot of the sheriff's office.

"We appreciate all the help you can give." He glanced around the reverend at two solidly built men. "We're going to search the woods around the lake. A few men in boats will patrol the lake." Hopefully, they wouldn't find them drowned or dead, just lost. "A chopper is going up in fifteen minutes."

Bishop nodded. "You are very thorough, agent."

"Deputy. Please step over to the sheriff's jeep and choose the area you'd like to search on the map."

"The area around my community is perfect." Bishop and his bookends headed for the jeep.

"That man is a pest," Pinson said, handing Everis a backpack. "He hard sells that church of his. I've had several complaints from folks around town."

"I'll talk to him." Just as soon as he had time. The missing girls took priority over a zealous preacher.

By the time the sun peeked over the mountain, cars were pulling out of the parking lot and headed for their respective search areas. Everis joined a group of men bound for the west side while Shar joined another. Four groups, each member of the sheriff's office assigned to one to keep the volunteers from scattering like chickens.

Everis parked his car and stepped onto the gravel pullout on the side of the road. He'd chosen a popular hiking area to explore and stepped close to the cliff, ducking under the crime scene tape. "The rest of you spread out and follow the trail," he ordered, glancing at the water below.

Nothing looked disturbed since the last time he was there. If the girls had stopped here to hang, or out of nosiness, their footprints would have been fresh. No one disappeared without a trace.

He turned and headed through the brush, following the trail, but keeping close to the cliff. Lauren and Megan wouldn't be the first teenagers to fall over the side. He hoped they hadn't been the most recent.

A shout came from up ahead. Everis sprinted to where two men stood around a dark patch of dirt. Splotches of what looked like blood dotted surrounding rocks.

He removed a small forensic kit from the pack on his back and squatted next to one. With a small knife he scraped off a sample and dropped it into a plastic baggy, then photographed the scene and sent the photos to Amber to print off. "You men, step back. This is now a potential crime scene." The blood looked too old to be from one of the girls, but he'd have to have the sample checked.

Dropping the baggy into his pack, he stood and surveyed the area. The men in his group looked on silently, waiting for orders.

"Let's look for more clues," he said. "If this does belong to one of the girls, we'll find more evidence."

After another hour of searching, they found nothing. No blood, no personal items, no clothing. It was as if whoever, or whatever, the blood belonged to had seeped into the ground.

Everis sent the men home and continued down the trail, meeting up with Shar, who was headed toward him. "Found blood, but I doubt it belongs to either girl."

"We found bones down below, which I'm pretty sure belongs to a deer. That blood is most likely from a poached deer kill."

Everis sighed. "Which puts us back at the beginning. Again." He picked up a nearby rock and threw it over the cliff.

"I'll meet you back at the office." She placed a

comforting hand on his shoulder. "We'll find something."

He nodded and returned the way he'd come. A chopper whirled overhead, flying in slow, ever-widening circles. He knew with certainty they wouldn't find anything either.

By the time he reached his car, all the others had gone. The crime scene tape had pulled free of a bush and now waved in the breeze. Everis pulled down the rest. Unless Jane Doe woke up, this was a dead end too.

He drove back to the office where Shar and the other two deputies waited in the conference room. Shar stood in front of a case board and tacked up a photo of the bones pulled from the lake. Next to those were photos of Jane Doe and the missing girls. Everis added his photo of the blood.

"Next time we do a search," Pinson said, "someone else gets to go with the talkative Reverend Bishop."

Shar smiled. "Still pressuring you to attend his church?"

"Yeah. Said I'd make a fine addition to the survivors in the new world and would produce many children. The man gives me the creeps. Have you ever spent a lot of time with him or been approached by him and his female clones? I have too many times. It's weird how the women walk with their heads down, not making eye contact. And all those daughters? What? Did his wife spend her entire adulthood pregnant?"

"Let's focus on the missing girls," Everis said. But he had thought the same things…strange.

"Focus on what?" Mayfield asked. "We don't have anything. They went to school, they left school, they said goodbye to their friend, Sara, then vanished."

"Alien abduction?" Pinson shrugged. "Just throwing that out there."

"Well, don't." Shar turned back to the case board. "Someone, bring Scott McIlroy in for more questioning."

Mayfield pushed to his feet. "You want me to pull him out of school?"

"Yep."

Everis's cell rang. "Deputy Hayes."

"We flew over that entire area. Didn't see anything out of the ordinary, other than the sprawling compound of that new preacher."

"Thanks." Everis hung up. "The chopper was another dead-end."

"We'll find something," Shar said, still staring at the board. "Eventually, something always gives."

The bad thing about that was they were approaching that critical first forty-eight-hour period when cases turned cold.

※ ※ ※

The reverend paced back and forth in front of the new girls. "Did you watch the orientation video?"

"What do you want with us?" The brunette asked.

"You are only allowed to answer the question asked."

"Yes." She gripped the hand of the girl next to her.

"Did it frighten you?"

They nodded.

"Good. You've been selected to survive in the new world." He patted the girl's cheek. "You'll fulfill your destiny as mothers and be fruitful."

They glanced at each other. "We're only seventeen."

"The perfect age."

"Can our families come?"

"I'll give that some thought. In the meantime, you'll be trained and taught a woman's proper place in the world. To disobey is to be punished severely. You'll now return to your room and reflect on what you've learned."

"Please." Tears ran down the redhead's face. "Let us go."

He waved his hand for them to be taken away and returned to his office. He closed the door to shut off their pleas. They'd learn. Some took longer than others, but they always learned their place. In his office, he removed the panel in the wall that let him watch the girls unobserved.

They sat on the edge of their cot, beautiful in their simple white gowns. Cleansing tears streaked their lovely faces. Lovely brides for some worthy men.

Chapter Five

"I don't understand why I'm here." Scott McIlroy folded his hands on the metal table in the interrogation room.

Shar locked gazes with him. "I get the feeling you weren't entirely honest with us about Megan."

He frowned. "I was. I swear."

Shar stared until the boy fidgeted, and beads of sweat formed on his upper lip. "Talk to me, Scott."

"Okay. We had a fight at lunch. She thought I was messing around on her. I wasn't. Anyway, I told her if she didn't stop making a scene, she'd be sorry. She threw her lunch tray at my head." He softly banged his head on the table. "There were tons of people who heard us."

The entire senior class was her bet. "We'll be asking questions."

"I know. Can I go now?"

"Yes." She stood and shook hands with the boy's father. "Thank you for your assistance."

"He didn't do anything, sheriff."

CYNTHIA HICKEY

She gave a thin-lipped smile and followed them from the room. She didn't think the boy had anything to do with the disappearance either, but his watching them from his bedroom window left enough suspicion for her to question him and the other students.

She stopped by Everis's desk. "I'm headed to the high school. Want to come?"

"Sure." He shut his laptop and followed her outside.

Their first stop was the principal's office. Mr. Dill was more than eager to help and made an announcement that the seniors would be pulled from class one-by-one. "You can question them in those rooms to the right of the auditorium.."

"We appreciate that, thank you." Shar headed for the room, taking the first student with her. "Have a seat, please. I'm Sheriff Camenetti and this is Deputy Hayes. I hope you don't mind if we record this?"

The girl crossed her arms. "I'm underage. Don't you need one of my parents here?"

"The office obtained that through phone calls and texts. Your name, please." This girl wasn't going to be easy.

"Ashley Lanson, straight A student. I don't know anything about Megan or Lauren, other than they thought they were all that and a bag of chips."

"You didn't like them?"

"Hardly anyone liked them."

"Don't you mean *likes*?" Shar straightened. "We don't know that anything bad has happened to them."

"I meant likes."

"Where do you live?"

"Not by them."

Shar raised an eyebrow. "Address."

Ashley gave her address.

"Do you drive, ride the bus, or walk?"

"The bus." She sighed and sank down in her chair. "My parents won't buy me a car."

"Get a job and buy one yourself. We're finished. Please exit through that door." Shar could check easily enough whether Ashley was on the bus after school that day. She got up and ushered in the next student.

By the tenth teen with an attitude, she pitied teachers and was totally onboard with them demanding a higher salary. "Name?"

"Roland Benson." The boy's eyes were a light hazel, in contrast with his dark skin. Perfect white teeth flashed in a face the color of creamed coffee. "I think you're wasting your time questioning us. You need to check with that preacher guy."

Shar narrowed her eyes. "Why?"

He leaned forward. "I take college classes on religion and have learned quite a bit about cults. Pretty little things like Lauren and Megan are just what those types are looking for."

"Expand on type." Shar sat back in her chair.

"Well, this Bishop fellow is getting ready for the end of the world, right? He's wanting to populate his community with survivors. What better way than to take healthy young girls and brainwash them?"

"You are a smart man, Roland Benson. Have you considered law enforcement?"

"I have." He grinned. "I want to join the FBI."

"I wish we would have met you the first day. You've given us the best scenario yet." She stood and offered her hand. "Good luck."

41

Once they'd questioned the last student and determined the five hottest girls in school were also the least popular, Shar was ready to strangle Mira. She explained her conversation with Roland to Everis.

"Looks like attending that church just became a priority. Those girls were bullies," he said. "We can't discount one of their peers doing something to them."

"We won't." Shar pulled Mira from school, dropped Everis off at the office, then took the girl home. "We need to have a talk."

"I told Everis I don't know what happened to Lauren and Megan. I wouldn't hurt my friends."

Shar cut her a quick glance as they walked up to the house. "You weren't that close, were you? I thought you still hung out with your old crowd."

"Not so much. Those girls are popular."

"Not really." Shar unlocked the front door. "Sit." She pointed to the kitchen table.

"Can't I get something to drink first?"

"Make it fast."

Mira mumbled something about interrogating innocent people and pulled a soda from the fridge. "What?" she asked, taking a seat.

"Attitude." Shar sat across from her. "I want to talk to you about you and your new friends' bullying. Because of that, Lauren and Megan weren't very well-liked except by those who wanted to get close to them."

"Like me."

"Did they bully you?"

"No, they asked me to join them." Mira twirled her soda can on the table. "It's not that we're bullies. We just rule the school. People get out of our way in the halls, give us the best table at lunch, let us cut in line…that kind of stuff."

"Or what?"

Mira refused to meet her gaze. "We spread rumors on social media."

Nausea rolled in Shar's stomach. Mira wasn't her daughter. She was still in school, but of legal age. She really couldn't tell the girl what to do. "Do you not realize that people commit suicide because of cyber bullying?"

"They didn't kill themselves. They aren't the type."

Shar closed her eyes and counted to ten. "That's not my point. Let me cut to the chase. If I hear of you bullying anyone again, I'll lock you up. Now, if we're finished treating you like the child you're acting like, I have some other mean girls to find."

* * *

Everis stepped into the sparse atrium of a church occupying an abandoned storefront. He supposed it wasn't abandoned anymore, although there seemed to be little improvements made. His boots beat out a rhythm on the well-worn floorboards.

When he stepped into the makeshift sanctuary, men and women in simple drab clothes turned to stare. No one looked to be over the age of forty.

The reverend marched down the aisle, a big grin on his face. "Agent Hayes. Welcome." He took Everis's hand and pumped it three times. "Please, take a seat on the right. That is where the men sit. We can't have any distractions." He waved a hand toward an empty seat in the front row.

"It's Deputy Hayes now." Why did the man insist on calling him by his prior title? What had Everis gotten himself into? He forced a smile and took his seat. Not that he had attended many church services, but this one seemed abnormally silent. Didn't most parishioners murmur when a stranger walked in?

"Please stand and recite our mantra." Bishop had taken his spot behind the podium.

As one, the congregation stood and recited, "God is good, we are one, what is ours is his, blessed be the name. The end is coming. We are to prepare. We are God's chosen." Then, they sat in unison.

Okay. Everis did his best to keep an impassive expression on his face, wishing he could slip on a mask as Shar did when the situation warranted her to keep her emotions and thoughts hidden.

For the next hour, the reverend spouted off nonsense pertaining to the "mantra," encouraging everyone there to convince others of the approaching peril and the safety of community. The man's face reddened and raised his voice as he tried to make his point that nothing was more important than a strong community.

Sounded like a scam to Everis. Who in the world was dumb enough to turn over all their possessions to a stranger in order to obtain eternal life? Nope. This was not the religion his mom had taught him about a long time ago.

After the service finally droned to a close, Everis tried to make a quick getaway. Not happening.

The reverend called his name. "We sure hope you join us again."

"I don't usually have Sundays off," he lied, "but when I do…"

"Wonderful. You must come out and visit our

community sometime. We've a chapel there as well, but it's our people that evoke the best spiritual awakening." He handed Everis a flier. "I think your eyes will be opened."

"I'll do so at my first opportunity." He gave a nod and almost sprinted for the door. His flesh crawled. He could feel Bishop's stare. Once free of the building, he headed to Shar's house. She'd agreed to watch Brian while he investigated.

She smiled from the porch at Brian running around the front yard after the mastiff, Goliath. Maybe Everis should get his son a dog. "Good morning." He ruffled Brian's hair, then rushed to kiss Shar.

"That's a nice greeting." She beamed up at him.

"There's plenty more where that came from." He sat in the rocker next to her.

"So, did the good reverend convert you?"

"Hardly. The man's theories are way out there."

She frowned. "How so?"

"It's all about the money and coming together against the end of the world and nonbelievers. I think he's a conspiracy theorist and perhaps a prepper who pulls the gullible in with him." He shuddered "He creeps me out."

"Prepper? As in a person who hoards food and supplies for the end of the world?"

"Yeah." He shrugged. "He's invited me to visit his community. Want to come along?"

"Now?"

"No. Tomorrow?"

"Sure, if he'll let me step foot on his property. Other than our first introduction, he acts as if I'm invisible."

He leaned over and kissed her, relishing the feel of

her soft lips on his and the scent of her flowery shampoo. "Maybe he's intimidated," he whispered.

She smiled under his kiss, then pulled back. "Not likely. The man exudes confidence."

Unlike his family. That nagging feeling spiraled down his spine. The man creeped him out. "Come on." Everis grabbed Shar's hand. "Let's take the kids for pizza."

Soon, Everis sat at a table with his son, Shar, Mira, and little Robby in his carrier. The parlor smelled of yeast and tangy tomato sauce. A server brought Brian a small mound of dough to form into any shape he wanted. This again was how Everis wanted to spend the rest of his life.

He lifted his glass of soda and studied Shar over the rim. She wasn't perfect, her lips a bit too full, her eyes almost too piercing, but she was the most beautiful woman he'd ever seen inside and out. She already struggled with her career and motherhood. Would she add wife to the mix?

"What?" She frowned.

"Nothing." He smiled. A noisy pizza parlor wasn't the place to discuss his feelings for her. Oh, she loved him, of that he was sure. They just hadn't had the right time to have that particular discussion.

Brian tugged on his sleeve, diverting Everis's attention to what he thought might be a teddy bear in the dough. "That's wonderful."

"It's you, Daddy. I'm going to eat you." His son's grin melted his heart. "With sauce!"

"Yes, with sauce," Shar chuckled.

"Ha ha." Everis grabbed her hand and took a playful nip. "Perhaps a bit of sauce on you."

Her eyes widened as Reverend Bishop and his skittish wife, who stuck close to his side as they entered the parlor. Rather than order, they moved from table to table handing out invites to church.

Shar narrowed her eyes as the reverend passed their table without a glance in her direction. In fact, he passed by all tables of middle-aged and older people. "I'm too old."

"What?" Everis's gaze followed the man and his wife.

"For his attention. I'm too old. He's only approached younger people and those with families."

"We have a family." His attention returned to her.

"A very mixed family and not biological. At least not with me." Was he really focusing on those of breeding age and those had proven they could father children? "I definitely want to visit his property tomorrow."

* * *

The next morning with Mira at school and the little ones at day care, Shar drove her and Everis to the Land of Superior Essence, or so the sign said on the gate they drove through. Two men with rifles stood on each side of the gate and watched them park. "What's he protecting?"

"No idea, but I intend to find out." Everis glanced in the sideview mirror.

Several buildings dotted the landscape. Most were two-stories high and resembled apartment buildings or army barracks. Clothes flapped from lines behind the structures. Women carried buckets from a well. The scene was like a peek into the past.

Men wore serviceable brown, black, or navy pants

with light-colored shirts. The women wore cheap cotton dresses that fell below their knees. "I feel as if I've stepped into Amish country without the hats, *kapps*, and pretty houses," Shar said, turning off the jeep's engine.

"Maybe that's what Bishop offers…a simpler life."

"That would be an attraction to some people." She actually enjoyed her small town not-so-simple life, but everyone had a right to live the way they chose. "There's a chapel. Why doesn't he hold his services there?"

"Town is more convenient maybe." Everis exited the jeep. "Are you coming?"

"Yeah." Shar slid from the jeep. The place reminded her of a nightmare she'd had as a child. One where robots ruled the world and she'd been the only human trying to act as if she belonged.

Heads turned as they made their way toward the building at the end of the dirt-packed path between what Shar guessed were the community living quarters. "Everyone here is blond." She stared at a group of young women washing laundry in a large metal tub. "Blond, unsmiling, and eerie as a forest on a night with no moon."

Reverend Bishop stepped from the last building before they reached it. His beaming smile was focused on Everis. It was as if Shar didn't exist. "Welcome, Agent Hayes."

Fine. Women had no authority in his world, but Shar *was* the authority in Highland Springs.

"Reverend, it's Deputy Hayes." Everis gave a nod. "Sheriff Camenetti and I would like a tour."

The man's face darkened, and his gaze flicked to Shar before returning to Everis. "You'll see that we do things differently here. Women are submissive to the men, as stated in the Good Book."

"The Bible?"

"Our improved version of that book." The man frowned at Shar, then turned. "Follow me. Please do not set a bad example for my women. They have accepted their roles."

Shar had an almost irresistible urge to create a scene. She bit her lip and ducked her head to hide a grin.

Everis bumped her with his shoulder. "Behave," he whispered.

"Yes, massah." She giggled, eliciting a glare from the good reverend. "My apologies."

"This building to our right is for our single men. The one across from it is our single women's. The larger building is for our married families." Bishop pointed as they walked. "As you can see, we've returned to our roots, doing things in the ways of our forefathers. When life as we know it ends, it will be these skills that will enable us to survive."

"Ends?" Shar asked, quickly adding, "Sorry. Everis, you ask him."

Bishop drew a sharp breath through his nose.

"Excuse her, sir. When the world ends?" Everis threw Shar a wink.

"All the signs are here. High unemployment, more frequent solar flares, more homeless and hungry, illness is on the rise...you name it, Deputy. The world is coming to an end. Look how severe our natural disasters have become. Only the prepared will survive what is coming." He faced Everis. "We'd love having a man like you in our midst."

Everis glanced around. "It seems as if my dark hair is out of place here."

"We thought at first that we were being called to a pure race, but we have realized it's a person's strength that matters. The purity of a person comes from within, not from his coloring. Purity is something that can be taught and embraced."

"The sheriff is one of the strongest, most honest people I've ever met. You can't get much better than that."

"Perhaps." The reverend continued the tour. "We need women of breeding age to repopulate the new world. It is nothing personal against the sheriff."

Shar rolled her eyes. The man was off his rocker. She held back, letting him and Everis stay a few feet ahead of her.

From the corner of a building, she caught a glimpse of a young girl watching. When she noticed Shar's attention, she drew back out of sight. Shar stared at the women at the well, then peered through the window of a nearby building. Children of all ages were seated at wooden desks while a young woman wrote on a chalkboard at the front of the room. Not one child seemed to be over the age of ten, and most were female.

She studied the women at the well again. They ranged in age from sixteen to twenty-five. Who was the young woman peeking around the building? Where were the older boys? She moved between the buildings and peered into a room on the other side of the school.

Cribs lined the walls. Cribs with pink blankets. Not a blue one in sight. Did they separate them so young? No, there were a few tow-headed boys in the school.

A lump rose in Shar's throat and threatened to

choke her. Something evil was going on. Something that would shake Highland Springs worse than anything it had experienced before.

"Sheriff." Bishop glared from the pathway. "If you please." He waved his arm for her to come.

"I'm sorry. I thought someone called me." She hurried past him, refusing to meet his eyes until she had slipped her sheriff mask into place. Then she faced him. "I'm very interested in learning more about your community, Reverend. I'll be keeping a close eye on this place. Perhaps a new world is definitely something to watch for."

A muscle ticked in the man's jaw. Good. He'd accepted her challenge.

Chapter Six

The reverend stormed through his front door. "Get that woman off my back." How dare she threaten him! Keep an eye on the community? He laughed, almost wishing she were of baby-birthing age. She had maybe one or two good years, but then worthless. Her spirit would definitely be something to pass along to the next generation. How he wished he could be the one to teach her a woman's proper place.

"Who?" His son glanced up from the newspaper he held in his hand.

"The sheriff."

"Why? I like her. She's gorgeous. That mane of black hair, silky skin—"

"All right, I get it." He narrowed his eyes. "You want her?"

"Yes." His son folded the paper and set it on a side table. "I have wives who are nothing but baby-making machines. I want a woman who is my equal, even if she doesn't give me a child."

The reverend fell into his chair. "The whole purpose

of all this is to repopulate and give you a world to rule."

His son shrugged. "She'll give me something. At least one. Then, in my old age, I'll have someone I can actually talk to."

The reverend made a noise in his throat. "She won't come willingly. I saw it in her eyes. She thinks this is all nonsense."

"Then she'll have to learn the hard way." He flexed his shoulders and winced before stepping out of the room.

Yes, he was hard on his son, but someday his son would have to take over the role of leader. He had to be disciplined, orderly, strong. He drummed his fingers on the arm of the chair. His son desired Sheriff Camenetti. He hadn't seen that coming. Perhaps it would be up to the reverend to see exactly what the woman was made of before his son made an irreversible move that would bring things tumbling down around them.

He pressed a button on the intercom next to him. "Send me Megan."

"Which one?" a man asked.

"The newest one!" Imbecile. Why would he want his first wife? Skinny and pouty, absolutely no fire left in her. He ought to rid himself of her. She was long past childbearing. Her only use was to help keep the girls in line and maintaining the façade of a pastor's only wife to a world blinded by false rules.

Sara number five entered, clutching a white robe tightly around her. She stood in front of him, eyes downcast.

"Disrobe and follow me." He stood and held out his hand.

She let the robe fall and slipped her small hand into

his.

* * *

Shar stood on her back porch, coffee in hand, and let Goliath out to run a bit before she headed to work. She'd tossed and turned the night before, replaying what she'd seen at the community. Something was horribly wrong there. As sheriff, it was up to her to find out what, while searching for the missing girls. When had her life become so busy?

"Come on, boy."

The twitch of Goliath's ear told Shar he heard her, but rather than obey as he usually did, he stayed focused on the trees behind her house. Mastiffs rarely barked, but even from where she stood, she heard the growl deep in his throat.

She set her mug on a rickety metal table and padded barefoot down the wooden steps to the dog's side. "What is it, boy?" She focused on the forest, one hand on Goliath's head.

He turned his head toward the house.

Shar's heart stopped. She trusted the dog's instincts more than her own. Without another thought, she dashed into the house and into Robby's room. The baby cooed happily, then grinned up at her when he caught sight of her. She scooped him into her arms and checked on Mira and Candy. Both were shuffling from their rooms, readying themselves for the day.

Candy frowned. "What's wrong with you?"

"Look at Goliath."

The dog had followed Shar into the house and now stared at the front door, his nose inches from the wood.

"Take the baby." Shar handed Robby to her sister, then took her gun from the hook on the wall near the door. "Go into the bedroom and lock the door. You go too, Mira."

Shar plastered her back against the wall and peered sideways through a slit in the curtains. No one stood on the front porch. There were no other vehicles in the driveway but her jeep and Candy's Sonata. Her gaze flicked back to Goliath, who hadn't relaxed his stance.

She took a deep breath and unlocked the door, then waited. When no sound came from the outside, she turned the handle and swung the door open. She leaped in the doorway, gun at the ready. Nothing. Nobody. She stepped onto the porch.

"Oh." A small cardboard box sat on the seat of her rocking chair. No way in Hades was she going to touch or open the thing. "Come on, boy. Let's call Everis."

Fifteen minutes later, Everis roared into the driveway, then bounded up her steps. He cast her a concerned look, then stared at the package. "I have a bomb squad coming from Hot Springs. They'll be here within thirty minutes."

"I hope it isn't a bomb. Oh, the others are locked in the bedroom." She hurried inside to ask them to head to their respective job and school. "Would you drop Robby off?" she asked Candy. "I've got to stay and see that the package is taken care of."

Candy nodded. "Be careful, sis. This is becoming the norm, and I don't like it."

"Neither do I." She yearned for the peace Highland Springs once had.

When the bomb squad arrived, she and Everis were ordered to stand at the edge of her property with Goliath. Five minutes later, the box was declared free of explosives.

Everis handed Shar a pair of vinyl gloves. "Are you going to open it?"

"Might as well." She headed back up the stairs and used the pocket knife Everis handed her to slit the tape holding the box closed. The flaps fell open to reveal the bloody stump of what looked like a woman's pinkie finger. "I sure wish our Jane Doe would wake up. I think this is all connected to her somehow."

"Gut feeling?"

"Yep." She pulled a folded slip of paper from the box and read, "Careful what you seek, sheriff, and where you dig."

"What the hell does that mean?" Everis glared.

"It's obviously a threat of some kind. Someone wants to play games."

"Then, let's play. Go get dressed and meet me at the office." Everis hurried to his car and sped away. He trusted Shar's instincts and agreed with her in this instance. Jane Doe, the community, the missing girls, and the package were all somehow connected.

His cell phone rang. He answered over blue tooth. "Deputy Hayes."

"It's Pinson. Someone walked into Jane Doe's room as slick as a weasel and cut off her finger."

"That's one question easily answered."

"What?"

"I'll explain when I get there." Everis hung up and sped to the office.

In no time, Everis made a pot of coffee, knowing Shar preferred the fancy stuff, but not having stopped to pick any up, he had a mug poured and in her place in the conference room. The other two deputies already sat at the table.

Shar walked in and took her seat, then glanced around the room. "What happened?"

"Someone cut off Jane Doe's finger." Pinson shook his head. "Had to be someone from the hospital, or disguised, because they moved right past the security guard outside her door. They didn't discover the deed until a nurse went in to check her vitals. By then, Jane Doe had lost a lot of blood."

"Is she still alive?" Shar reached for her coffee. "Thanks."

"Yep, so is the baby."

"I want you and Mayfield to take over guard duty. We can't lose this woman. She's the key to what's going on here," she said.

"What is going on here?" Pinson glanced from her to Everis.

"We're not sure. That's why we need Jane Doe to wake up."

Shar pulled the box from her pocket and slid it across the table. "I got the finger as a present. Want to take that away for me?"

Pinson paled. "That's sick."

"I thought Townsend and his social media killings were bad." Mayfield shuddered. "I hope you aren't going to receive a body piece-by-piece."

"At least the finger doesn't belong to Lauren Helms or Megan Tims," she said.

Everis wanted to head to the Land of Superior Essence and shake something up. But he couldn't act on a feeling. They needed proof. It was quite possible Bishop was just a nut, and had nothing to do with Jane Doe. Still, the drabness of the woman's nightgown was too similar to what the other community women's garb for the idea to be pushed aside.

"What's the plan?" Mayfield asked. "Other than guard duty?"

Everis glanced at Shar. "I'm going to become very close friends with Reverend Bishop."

Shar nodded. "I'll work on finding out information about our Jane Doe. Her prints aren't in the system, and no one has come forward as to her identity. I'm going to expand where we send her photo and check with DMV in surrounding states. Someone knows this girl."

"Right." Everis stood. "I'm off to visit my new best friend on the pretense of wanting to know more." Not much of a pretense; he definitely wanted to know more.

He drove to the building in town where they held church, hoping Bishop had an office there. He didn't. The place was locked up as tight as a pickle jar. Everis stood on the sidewalk and scanned the street. The man and his group of women had been seen every day going from one business to the other. If he could find them, he could tag along and listen to their spiel.

He left his car parked on the curb and headed one street over where there were more places open for business. Highland Springs's main business section consisted of streets lined up like a hashtag symbol. After that, the sporadic businesses stretched down the road leading to the interstate.

He found the group entering the town's newspaper office. With a population of three thousand, The Highland Gazette only put out a weekly paper. Everis pushed open the door and entered behind Bishop and the women.

"Good afternoon, sir." Bishop thrust out his hand to

the editor. "I'm Reverend Bishop of the Church of Superior Essence. This is my wife and daughters. I'd like to extend a personal invitation to join us for this Sunday's service."

The editor scowled. "Sounds like a cult to me."

Bishop's smile never faded. "Not in the slightest, sir. We're a group of god-fearing people who are preparing to enter into a new world. A world where only a chosen few will survive. We'd like for you to be one of them."

The editor still hadn't returned the reverend's handshake. Instead, he crossed his arms and shook his head. "Nope. I'm Freewill Baptist and don't aim to change. Thanks anyway."

Bishop dropped a flier on the counter. "Should you change your mind." He turned to leave and spotted Everis. His smile turned genuine. "Deputy Hayes. What a pleasant surprise."

"Mind if I join you?"

"Not at all!" He sauntered from the office, chest swelled. "I thought it might be a good thing to have a newspaper editor in our new world, but the man is older than I originally thought. We need hearty young people to form our world. Wouldn't you agree?"

"Sure." Everis glanced at the man's wife.

She refused to meet his gaze, focusing on the sidewalk instead. As did the five young women next to her. If they really were his daughters, his wife had to have been consecutively pregnant for five years.

"Might I make a suggestion? I'd hate to step over any boundary lines, but if you want to entice people, it might help if your family looked a bit...happier? Smiled and made eye contact with the people you approach?"

"Have my wife and daughters speak to strange men?" He took a step back. "Immoral."

"They don't have to touch them, just smile and hand out fliers. Very few people can resist a pretty girl." Besides, those poor things would turn away a hungry bear with their downcast expressions.

Bishop rubbed his chin. "That definitely deserves a thought. Thank you, Deputy. You're a forward-thinking man. I'm happy you found us. Shall we move on? There's a bakery up ahead."

"Only if you let me treat your family to doughnuts." It was too easy to make friends with this man.

Chapter Seven

Dressed as a landscaper, this time in a bright yellow vest and carrying a leaf blower, he watched the girl, Mira, leave school and head for the bad part of town. If she was still hanging with her gangster boyfriend, the reverend might think her unworthy of saving. Still, there was something about her that made the man think her worth the trouble.

He waited for her to turn the corner, then flipped off the blower and followed. The girl walked with purpose, veering off toward the park. Yes, she was meeting her boyfriend. The man watched from behind a tree.

It soon became obvious Mira was breaking up with the boy, if his angry expression was any indication. She put a hand on his arm, then turned and walked away. Perfect. She would be occupied with her thoughts and not paying attention to her surroundings. He waited until the boy headed away, then followed Mira.

"Hey!"

He spun around to see the young man sprinting

toward him. The man swerved and dashed through the apartment complex. If he were caught, he'd have more explaining to do than he could answer and live to see another day.

Shar glanced up from her desk, surprised to see Mira and JoJo standing in the doorway. "What's up?"

JoJo approached the front of her desk, arms folded across his chest. "I caught some white man following Mira."

"Mira?"

"I went to the park to break up with JoJo," she cleared her throat, "and the next thing I know, JoJo is yelling at some man in a construction vest."

Shar set down the ink pen she was using to brainstorm with. "How do you know he was following Mira?" She locked her gaze on JoJo's dark one.

"Why else would he be there?" He crossed his arms.

"Working?" She sighed. "I'm not going to disregard your story. Not with girls still missing, but we have to make sure before we accuse anyone. Also, I don't want you chasing down a potential suspect. You could be killed."

"I'm not afraid."

"You should be. Can you describe this man?"

"White, a little taller than me. I could have caught him if he hadn't hid like a girl."

"Did you see his face? His hair color?"

"He had on a blue baseball cap."

Shar stood. "I'll take you home, Mira. I don't want you out alone. We'll discuss your ditching school later." She needed to discuss with her deputies whether a curfew needed to be enforced on the town. What could she say? Lauren and Megan disappeared in broad daylight together. "Do you need a ride, JoJo?"

"I'd like to see my son." He ducked his head.

Shar's suspicions six months ago were true. This young man was Robby's father. "Then come on."

She dropped the two off at the house where Candy was home with Robby, then drove to the park. She didn't really expect to see anything, but texted Everis to meet her there anyway.

Propped against the tree was a leaf blower. Shar snapped some vinyl gloves over her hands and stashed the garden tool in the back of her jeep. She doubted they'd find any fingerprints, but sometimes they got lucky.

She closed the jeep as Everis drove up. "There's no way of knowing whether JoJo saw the man who was our abductor, but there's nothing to say he isn't," she said. "He again dressed as a city worker with a blue baseball cap."

"Sounds like a close enough description to make me concerned." He tilted her face to his. "Don't be worried. We'll keep Mira safe."

"What about the other girls in this town? Everis, we have a lot of teenage girls attending that high school. We can't escort them all home."

He stepped back and glanced toward the apartment complex. "Can we extend the bus route to cover those who live in town? That way, either students are picked up or driven in a bus. No one walks home. Let's check out the complex."

Shar fell into step beside him. "I'll talk to the principal and head of the school board before returning to the office." The idea held merit and made more sense at this time than a curfew.

As was their normal welcome whenever they patrolled the apartment complex, windows fell into place, doors slammed, and suspected gang members stared with a fierce intensity. If not for JoJo, Shar wouldn't feel safe. As it was, adopting his son gave her a measure of respect among the apartment dwellers.

"You chasing a man in a yellow vest?" An elderly woman glanced up from her rocking chair outside her door.

"Yes, ma'am."

"He went that away. Most likely scaled the fence and went through the junkyard."

"Thank you." Suspecting the woman was right, Shar and Everis headed in that direction anyway.

"Gone." Everis shook the chain-link fence, then jumped back when a dog seemingly appeared out of nowhere and charged the fence. He grinned.

"What?" Shar glanced from him to the dog. "Oh, the dog knows our alleged abductor." The prior junkyard dog now lived with Shar. She couldn't image Goliath ever acting this ferocious despite his size.

"It does appear that way. Let's pay the junkyard owner a visit."

They hurried back to the jeep and drove to the junkyard gate. Shar laid on the horn until a man approached and told the frenzied dog to hush. With his hand on the animal's collar, he waved them in.

Shar rolled down her window. "I'm Sheriff Camenetti, and this is Deputy Hayes. We'd like to ask you a few questions."

"Drive on up to that building. I'll be there in a

minute."

Shar nodded and parked in front of a small metal trailer. Making sure there weren't any more dogs ready to attack, she climbed out of the jeep and waited for the owner to join them.

"I'm Doug Murphy. What can I do for you, sheriff?" He opened the trailer door and motioned for them to enter.

"We're looking for a man in a construction worker's yellow vest who was possibly seen running through here."

"Not possible." He sat behind a dented green, metal desk. "Brutus out there would have torn his face off."

"Unless the dog knew the man." Shar glanced around the sparse office.

Two hard plastic chairs sat against one wall. A tall filing cabinet took up a corner next to a Formica counter that held a microwave and coffeepot. "Do you work here alone?"

"I own the place." He folded his hands on the desk. "Look, sheriff. My dog is not a pet. He doesn't like anyone but me. I'm telling you there's no way someone ran through here without me telling Brutus it's okay."

"How do you do business with a dog like that?" Everis asked. "I'm sure customers aren't lining up at the gate."

"On the contrary, I do a fair amount of business. There's an intercom on the gate. Folks drive up, tell me what they want, and if I have something, I buzz them through and tell Brutus to be good."

"Any regular customers?"

The man twisted his mouth as he thought. "Yeah.

Recently, that new reverend and a couple of his guys have been coming by a lot for materials for that community of his."

Shar glanced at Everis, then back at Murphy. "Thank you. Please call us if you think of anything else." She handed him a business card, then left with Everis.

Back in the jeep, she said, "The dear reverend sure pops up a lot, doesn't he?"

"Yep. It might be time to question him a bit further." Everis held up a baggy. "Got a cigarette butt from outside the junkyard office. Let's get some fingerprints from Bishop and his goons and see if we can't lift some from that leaf blower."

"We need to visit the Highland Springs High first. School lets out in an hour."

At the school, the principal was more than willing to help. "I'll contact the bus administration immediately and send out an alert to all our parents. What about the elementary and junior high?"

"Let's play it safe," Shar said, "and follow the same procedure. I'd also like you to call an emergency assembly immediately. I want to talk to all students ages twelve and up. I'd also like a letter sent home with every student and posted on the website asking that no student walk home or be on the streets without adult supervision until further notice."

"Right away." Mr. Dill picked up the phone and gave instructions to his administrative assistant. Then, he flipped on the intercom and asked that all junior high and high school students convene immediately in the auditorium.

Fifteen minutes later, Shar stood in back of a

simple podium on the school stage and stared at a sea of curious teenage faces. The sight immediately thrust her back to her own teen years when she had stood on the same stage as valedictorian. While she still didn't enjoy public speaking, this was easier than a press release in front of television cameras.

A girl in the front row raised her hand. "Did you find Lauren and Megan?"

"Not yet." Shar gripped the edges of the wood podium. "I've asked all students to meet here so I can easily issue a warning. While we are not yet enforcing a curfew, we are strongly suggesting that no student walk home or be outdoors without adult supervision." She raised a hand as voices shouted in opposition. "I know you aren't children, but this is for your safety. It's just until we catch the person responsible for Lauren's and Megan's disappearance. If you are caught out, you will be picked up and taken home. Thank you."

With increasing cries of outrage, Shar exited the stage. "A lot of unhappy kids."

"That age doesn't often see the bigger picture," Mr. Dill said. "We can only hope they heed your advice."

Shar followed Everis from the school and back to the jeep. "Let's get the cigarette and lawn blower sent to the lab before heading out to question Bishop."

"We won't have to hunt the man down." Everis pointed to the sidewalk where Bishop and his ever-present family headed into the drugstore.

That was the second time since meeting the man that Shar had witnessed them in that store. "Do you think someone is ill? They seem to frequent that store a lot."

"We'll ask that question along with all the others." Everis closed the jeep door he'd just opened. "Let's get this over with."

Chapter Eight

"Good afternoon, Sheriff." Shar entered the drugstore ahead of Everis.

Bishop turned from the front counter, his usual large smile in place. "Good afternoon, Sheriff and Deputy Hayes. What brings you here on this fine day?"

Shar squared her shoulders, prepared for an argument. "We'd like to ask you a few questions down at the office if you don't mind."

Surprise flickered in his eyes, but he nodded. "That will be fine. Come along, ladies. We'll return for our prescription."

Fifteen minutes later, Shar and Everis asked the reverend's family to wait in the reception area. The five women stared wide-eyed at Amber's low cut dress and big hair. Trying not to show how funny the situation seemed to her, Shar escorted Bishop to the interrogation room.

With Everis next to her, she sat across from him at the metal table, hands folded in front of her. "Thank you for agreeing to a few questions. May we get you a soda, coffee, water?"

"I would enjoy a glass of water," he said.

Everis got up to fetch the glass. Shar smiled when he chose an actual glass rather than a paper cup they usually used.

"We're curious about the constant visits to the junkyard." Shar saw no other way to ask her questions other than straight out.

He stiffened in his chair. "It's no secret that we're building a community. A junkyard is an inexpensive place to find materials."

"True." She kept her smile in place. "It's my job to look out for the residents of Highland Springs, which you are. I've recently visited the junkyard along with Deputy Hayes. Has any of your people been injured by the dog?"

"That dog wouldn't dare." He leaned forward, keeping his gaze locked on Shar's. For once, the man seemed to respect her authority. "I tell him in a very firm manner to sit. He does. Animals, like people, just need to know who is in charge" His gaze shifted to Everis. "I'm sure a man like your deputy commands respect."

"As does the sheriff," Everis added. "She is well-respected in this town."

He gave a dismissive shrug and lifted the water glass to his lips. After taking a sip, he set the glass firmly onto the tabletop, then slid it toward Shar. "My fingerprints. That is why I'm here, am I correct? For some silly reason, I'm a suspect in the disappearance of those girls."

"No offense, Reverend, but we cannot leave anyone out of the investigation." Shar stood. "I'm sure you can understand that. What if one of the girls was one of your daughters?"

"I would move every rock." He stood too. "Feel free to ask the women of my community whether they are being held against their will." Back ramrod straight, he marched from the room.

His voice boomed down the hall as he told his women it was time to leave.

Everis rubbed his hands down his face. "If that man is guilty, he isn't going to be easy to crack."

"No, he isn't. I'm heading home for the unpleasant task of confronting Mira about skipping her afternoon classes. She's barely passing as it is."

"There isn't much you can do, Shar. She's eighteen."

Shar exhaled heavily. "But she is living under my roof, and that privilege comes with rules. Come by later for pie. I smelled Candy baking one when I dropped the kids off."

"That's the best thing I've heard all day."

"Here's something better. Come earlier than that and I'll make Italian." She flashed him a grin and headed home.

When she pulled into the drive, Goliath came to greet her. "Who let you out?" She scratched behind his ears and stepped onto the porch.

The front window curtains were parted, and she had a clear view of Mira, JoJo, and Robby. Kids having kids. The scene ripped at her heart. Until the final papers were signed on Robby's adoption, Shar could lose her son to his biological parents. She didn't think she could give him up without a fight, but she cared very much for Robby's mother too. With the weight of work and family on her shoulders, she entered the house.

Mira glanced up from her spot on the floor. "Time to pay for my crimes." She got up and moved to the sofa. "You'd better go, JoJo, before she lights into you too."

"I do not 'light' into anyone." Shar started to hang her weapon in its usual place high on the wall, glanced at JoJo and decided to keep it close. Robby wasn't old enough to worry about yet, and Mira wouldn't touch it because of her fear of guns. She said because her parents were shot and killed, but Shar never found any evidence of that story being true.

"I'll see you later, Mira. Glad you took me back." He gave Shar a thin-lipped smile, then dashed out the front door.

"Back together?" Shar hung up her gun.

"He loves Robby. He loves me. What's a girl to do?"

"Do you love him?" Shar sat next to her.

"I do, but I have big plans. I want more than a crappy apartment, a man who gets his money under the table, and a bunch of babies." She crossed her arms and rested her feet on the coffee table. "I want a real job where I can wear nice clothes like Amber."

Shar fought hard to keep from bursting out laughing. She wouldn't consider the tight clothes her receptionist wore to be nice, but everyone was entitled to their own opinion. "So, why did you skip school?"

She glanced at Shar as if she were dense. "To see JoJo. I thought that was obvious."

"It could have waited. You could have been abducted like your friends, and I wouldn't have known otherwise. I would have thought you were at school until two."

"I'm smarter than they are."

"You're still just a young woman and no match for a strong man. We have rules in this house, Mira. If you want to stay here, and I really hope you do, then you must abide by them." She told the girl what she'd spoken about in the assembly. "I know it's inconvenient, but it's to keep everyone safe."

Once Mira agreed not to go anywhere without her or Candy, Shar took a quick shower, changed into shorts and an oversized tee shirt, then headed to the kitchen to start supper.

Candy glanced up from the kitchen table. "You're home early."

"I'm cooking Italian."

Her sister grinned. "Everis must be coming."

"He is."

With a bottle of red wine in one hand and a six-pack of beer in the other, Everis entered Shar's house and took a deep breath. Tomatoes, onions, and garlic teased his senses. His stomach rumbled. He loved when Shar cooked Italian. "Come on, son," he told Brian. "You're about to get a new favorite food."

"This is every man's dream," he said, putting all but one beer in the fridge. "Two beautiful women cooking for him." He then wrapped his arms around Shar's waist and nuzzled her neck.

"No fair." Candy popped him with a towel.

He grinned her way. "Not when Shar is around."

"Oh, you two." Shar slid free of his embrace. "Make yourself useful and shred that lettuce."

"Gladly." Everis moved to the kitchen island, popped the top off his beer, and picked up the butcher knife. "Not a single young person roaming the streets tonight."

"I guess that means the party at the lake really is called off."

"Or they're being sneaky." He really hoped the kids took Shar's speech seriously and called off the party.

After supper, they all congregated in the living room. Brian played blocks with Robby, who squealed with joy every time the tower fell. Shar looked on with a tender expression on her face. Everis could get used to nights like this. There was nothing better than spending time with the most important people in his world.

Chapter Nine

The sheriff and her sidekicks were stupid. The man—he liked the sound of that and would continue to think of himself as such. After all, the reverend said if he proved himself worthy, he'd be the youngest elder in the community.

Now, here he sat, a beer in one hand, while he scoured the party for the next worthy girl. Perhaps one of the ones he took would be his wife. If he were able to choose a wife, it wouldn't be a skank like Megan or Lauren. Nope, he'd want someone pretty but smart, and a bit on the shy side. Someone like Carol.

With long light brown hair and hazel eyes that sparkled behind wire-rimmed glasses, she wasn't perfect, but he'd desired her from the first moment he saw her. He couldn't snatch her there. Too many people to cry the alarm. He'd have to bide his time. He knew with certainty the time would come.

He continued to study the crowd and smiled as a girl stepped into the bushes. Probably to relieve herself. She'd not be expecting him.

He skirted the perimeter of the clearing where the party was held. When Carol stood and pulled up her jeans, he clapped a hand over her mouth and dragged her away.

"You took her from a party?" The reverend frowned from his seat behind his desk. "That was risky."

"I know, but I told you I was up to any task you put before me."

The reverend studied the girl in front of him, her eyes wide behind her glasses. "She isn't perfect. There may not be a way to acquire glasses in the new world."

"I want her."

The girl squeaked under her gag and tried to make a dash for the door. The two guards stepped together and formed an effective barrier.

The reverend steepled his fingers under his chin. When had those he'd chosen to surround himself with taken to requesting whom they wanted as brides? He much preferred choosing for them, since God had given him discernment in such matters.

"I'm ready to be baptized into the community. I'm ready to take my role as an elder."

The reverend sighed. "Don't rush, my boy. There's time. We haven't completed our harvest, and you're needed in the field. Your work is vital for our survival." He stood and rounded his desk, laying a hand on the young man's shoulder. "Exercise caution. If caught, I cannot let on that I know you or asked this of you."

"You don't need to worry. I have a plan if I get caught, which I won't."

Shar's cell phone rang. She sat up, missing Everis's

arm around her shoulders almost immediately, and grabbed the phone from the coffee table. "Sheriff Camenetti."

"She just went to the bathroom." A girl sobbed on the other end. "She never came back."

"Who is it?" Everis mouthed.

Shar held up a finger. "Slow down. Who is this?"

"Amy Peterson."

"Where are you?"

"At the lake by the abandoned fishing shack. There's a lot of us here."

"Try not to let anyone leave. We're on our way." Shar hung up and bolted to her feet. "We have another disappearance." She grabbed her gun belt from the hook by the door.

"Shar." Everis grinned. "While I enjoy the view of your long legs, I don't think teenage boys could handle it."

"Darn it." She raced to the bedroom and hurriedly pulled on a pair of yoga pants, told Candy she had to go, then rejoined Everis.

"Still sexy, but at least you're covered." He locked the door behind them. "So they went ahead with the party."

"Appears that way." Why didn't kids listen? When she gave an order to stay home, it wasn't to be mean. It was to keep them safe. *Please, God, don't let someone be killing these girls.*

They sped to the party location. The group of about twenty sat around staring at the ground instead of having fun. Empty beer bottles poked from underneath bushes in a sorry attempt at hiding them, and a haze of marijuana smoke hung over it all like a curtain.

Shar wanted to slap them all in handcuffs and lock them up for their own protection. Instead, she glared. "Who's the girl who called me?"

Fingers pointed at a chubby brunette. The girl stepped forward. Mascara streaked her cheeks. "I'm Amy."

"Who is missing?"

"Carol."

"Did anyone else see Carol?"

Scott McIlroy stepped beside Amy. "We all did at the beginning. I didn't know she was missing until Amy started asking around. She went into the woods to pee and didn't come back."

"Did anyone see which way she went? How long has she been gone?" Shar crossed her arms. "Does anyone know anything?"

Amy started to cry. "I was making out with Luke. I remember Carol saying she had to go, but didn't pay attention to the time until it seemed like a really, really long time."

Shar clenched her jaw to keep from saying something mean. "Is anyone else gone that was here at the beginning?"

"A few people," Scott said. "They come and go. We don't have a set time for the party to end."

"You weren't supposed to have a party at all."

Everis clapped a hand on her shoulder. "I'll see if I can find anything in the woods."

"The rest of you have a seat. You aren't leaving without your parents."

"But our cars," someone shouted.

"Not my concern. Have a parent bring you back tomorrow. You are not leaving here without an adult, so start calling." There was no way she could keep these kids safe. All she could do was pretend and put on her sheriff mask. How could she fight a phantom?

Angry parents started arriving within half an hour, leading sheepish teens away. All except for Carol's. Her parents, Mr. and Mrs. Nelson clung to each other.

"You had no idea your daughter was attending this party?" Shar asked.

"No. She said she was spending the night with Amy." Tears rolled down the mother's face. "She's usually such a good girl."

"Attending a party doesn't make her bad. Our main concern now is finding her." Shar turned as Everis exited the woods.

He shook his head. "Some heel marks where she was probably dragged and prints from a shoe that most people probably own."

Shar studied the area again now that everyone except the distraught parents were gone. "Could it be someone who had attended the party?" Could they really be searching for a teenage abductor? The thought made her stomach roll.

"I'm starting to think the same thing," Everis said. "It's someone from the high school."

"But what about Bishop?"

"I still feel as if he's somehow involved, but he isn't the one abducting the girls. I'd bet my badge."

Shar's heart skipped a beat. "This might sound crazy, but what if these girls are being abducted for the sole purpose of being brainwashed into Bishop's cult?"

The thought made Everis's blood run cold. It was more imperative than ever that getting in with Bishop take priority. "How do you want to handle this?"

"I want a list of only male attendees at the school ages fifteen and up and I want prints of their shoes." She returned to the distraught parents. A few seconds later they shuffled to their vehicle.

That was going to be a huge job on limited manpower. It was time for them to call for help. If the Arkansas Federal Bureau of Investigations sent a couple of agents, it would free him and Shar up to infiltrate the cult. He pulled his phone from his pocket and made the call.

The disappearance of three young girls warranted them two agents who would arrive in the morning.

When morning came, Everis was on his second cup of coffee and running on little sleep. Shar, who had gone home to change into her uniform, didn't look much more rested, although she said she'd grabbed a catnap.

"When the agents arrive," she said, "I want them to visit every single teenage boy in this town. If that doesn't work, move up to the recently graduated. That leaves Mayfield and Pinson to carry on with the day-to-day of this office and you and I to investigate Bishop."

"Sounds like a good plan." Everis grimaced at the bitter coffee. "Whatever happened to the Keurig I bought six months ago?"

"Mayfield broke it."

"Then I'll buy another." He set his mug down. "I can't stomach this stuff. I swear it's like drinking battery acid."

"It's not that bad." She stood as two men in suits entered the conference room.

Everis grinned. He'd worked with Agent Mills and

Agent Rollins before. Young, but good men. "Sheriff Camenetti, meet Agent Mills and Agent Rollins."

They all shook hands and Shar filled them in on what had been happening.

Agent Mills frowned. "This Bishop sounds suspiciously like the group recently run out of Southern Arkansas. I can check into that for you."

"That would be wonderful," Everis said. "We're stretched too thin. Any help and/or ideas are more than welcome."

He pulled a small bottle from his pocket and shook two white capsules into his hand, handing Shar and Everis each one. "These contain a tracker. If you ever find yourself in trouble, swallow it. They're good until they…pass."

By the time the other two deputies stumbled into work, Everis felt confident they had a good plan in place. It wouldn't be a fast one, but if they were right about Bishop wanting the girls to grow his community, they weren't in any immediate danger. It gave him a small measure of comfort that they might not find dead bodies.

"I'd like to interview the parents of the missing girls, too," Agent Rollins said. "Sometimes they know more than they think. Also, this girl…" he flipped through the file, "Sara."

"Feel free to do whatever you feel is necessary," Shar said. "We'll meet at the beginning of each work day and at the end to fill each other in."

Everis hoped they'd have something new to share.

Chapter Ten

Reverend Bishop, hands clasped behind his back, strolled along the path of his domain. He was king here. Look at how the others bowed their heads before him. He would rule his new world with justice, mercy, and discipline.

His son rushed toward him. "We have a problem."

"What would a world be without problems?"

"I mean a real problem. One of the new converts wants out."

"That's not possible. The people are told that fact when they join and are baptized. Who is it?"

"Harvey Larson and family." Donald Junior fell into step beside him. "They're waiting for you in your office."

"As my heir, this is something you need to be a part of. Fetch the enforcers and join me immediately." Reverend Bishop marched into his office. Really nothing more than a metal desk, a worn chair, and two hard chairs across from him. It was the adjoining room where he actually practiced his dominion—the room the community residents feared.

The family of three stood in front of his desk. The father stood rigid, eyes straight ahead, the women's eyes were downcast. They were model citizens. Why want out?

The Reverend sat. "Why do you want out of a future that guarantees survival?"

"My daughter needs medical attention," the man said. "Something you deny her. Her breathing has worsened, not improved."

"Then your daughter is full of sin and lacking in faith. You signed over your worldly possessions and took an oath. There is no leaving." The Bishop stood and motioned to the men in the back of the room. "Bring them to the courtyard."

"No, please." The mother wailed and clutched her daughter. "She's a lovely girl. Forgive us. We want to stay."

Ignoring her pleas, the reverend led the way as the enforcers physically dragged the parents to the posts standing upright in the packed dirt. They were then tied to the posts, then stripped from the waist up. Each enforcer took a whip and glanced at the reverend.

"Twenty lashes each."

As the first lash hissed against her father's back, the daughter turned and fled.

The reverend motioned for a man watching from the sidelines to go after her. With a nod, he dashed away, returning minutes later with the girl, who visibly struggled to breathe.

"Stand her in front of her parents. They need to see what happens when people disobey and refuse to believe." The reverend lifted his chin.

The enforcer punishing the woman stopped and approached the girl. Grabbing her hair, he bent her head back, and with a quick flick of the knife he pulled from his belt, slit her throat and let her fall.

"May her blood be cleansed through the soil of our earth," the reverend said. "Let the parents hang there until nightfall." He headed back to his office, serenaded by the screams and moans of the Larsons.

* * *

Shar stood next to the bed of Jane Doe and stared at the bandage around her finger. "We sure do need you to wake up, young lady. We've a lot of questions that need answering."

"She's on the mend," the doctor said, stepping into the room. "Even better, the baby is doing well. Growing as it should. Jane Doe was a bit malnourished when she was brought in, but we've remedied that."

"Any idea when you'll bring her out of the coma?"

"I'm turning off that particular medication now. The rest is up to this little lady."

"Thank you. Please call me as soon as she wakes." Shar turned and left. Other than stalking the reverend and his family, she didn't have much to go on. She didn't know for sure that Jane Doe came from his community. They couldn't be the only group of women who wore modest white nightgowns, right?

Since it was Tuesday, she doubted anyone would be at the building where he held his church services. She left the hospital and headed there. It wouldn't hurt to comb the place with a trained eye. Easier to do when it was devoid of people.

To her surprise, the front door was unlocked.

Tacked to the door was a small sign that invited the passerby to come in and find composure in the peace of the sanctuary.

Her shoes tapped against the floor as she pushed through the swinging double doors that elicited a shrill squeak as they opened into the sanctuary. Everis had described the place to her, where the people sat, but she hadn't been prepared for the quiet eeriness of the place. No peace filled her soul as was common in churches. Instead, the hair on her arms rose as she approached the podium. This was a place of evil.

She swallowed past a lump, threatening to seize her throat, and moved toward a door to the right of the podium, leaving the one on the left to explore later. She had to pass a baptismal font on the way and couldn't help but glance into the placid water. How easily some people were drawn to things that harmed them rather than helped. She opened the door and stepped into a storage room filled with boxes.

No choir robes like the ones stored in the church she'd attended as a child. A copper pot still held a few coins and bills from the weekend's collection. Definitely not enough to pay any church's expenses. Lined against a back wall were the type of boxes copy paper came in.

Shar had turned to leave when she heard a rasping noise. At first, she chalked it off to a rodent, but it sounded again, louder the second time. She unhooked the safety on her holster and put her hand on the butt of her gun. "This is Sheriff Camenetti. I strongly suggest you come out of there."

A young woman stepped from behind the boxes. Long blond hair had fallen free of its bun and hung down shoulders, covered in a pale blue dress dotted with yellow flowers. She wore dark socks that went past her knees, and heavy shoes. She peered from under her bangs. "Don't shoot."

"Of course, I won't shoot you." Shar relaxed. "What's your name?"

"My new name or the old one?"

"Let's go with the one you were born with."

"Annie Roper. I'm nineteen-years-old and joined the church right after my eighteenth birthday." Tears welled in her eyes. "That was the worst mistake I've ever made."

"Why?" Shar studied the girl's thin face. "I'm very interested in what—" the squeak of the swinging doors stopped her. "Get behind me."

Annie pressed so close to Shar's back they almost became one person. "Don't let them take me back. They'll kill me."

That was a statement that would need addressing at some point. As Shar reached to push the door closed, Everis stepped into sight. "Shar?"

"Thank goodness." She moved away from Annie. "We have a fugitive who is more than willing to talk."

He glanced toward the front of the building. "You'd better find a back way out of here. Bishop is right behind me."

Shar grabbed Annie's hand and darted through the door to the left of the baptismal, hoping it was an exit. They dashed through a room with a sofa and simple coffee table and out another door into the alley behind the buildings. "Stay close."

Keeping against the brick wall of the building, Shar led the girl to the end and peered around the corner at her jeep. The coast was clear. She turned and gripped Annie by the shoulders. "I need you to do exactly as I say. Do you understand?"

She nodded, blue eyes wide.

"Get behind that dumpster. Don't make a sound. Don't come out until you hear me call you." Once the girl had done as she was told, Shar sprinted around the corner, slowing her pace to a walk, in case anyone was watching. She climbed into the jeep without incident and drove down the alley.

Rolling her window down, she said, "Hurry, Annie."

The girl scampered from her hiding place and into the jeep, hunkering on the floorboards out of sight. Mouth set in a grim line, Shar drove to the sheriff's office.

* * *

"Were you talking to someone?" Bishop asked, joining Everis at the front of the sanctuary.

"Just myself. That's a lot of copy paper in there." He jerked his thumb toward the room Shar had exited.

Bishop grinned. "Don't become too nosy, Deputy. We all know what happened to the curious cat. Wait here while I get what I came for, then we'll head over to the fire station."

The Highland Springs rural fire department wasn't large, and Everis doubted any of the volunteer firemen would have any interest at all in Bishop's crazy scheme of survival. But the Ozarks were full of preppers. The Bishop might find someone close to his beliefs. He'd gathered his followers somewhere.

Had Shar found that girl in the storage room? Five minutes later, she would have been discovered.

Dangerous if she had escaped the community.

Everis wished he hadn't agreed to accompany Bishop this morning. He'd rather be there when Shar questioned the girl. Not following a pompous ass like some starstruck fan. But, and it was a huge but, he would do almost anything to bring this man down if he was up to something illegal that had to do with the missing girls. If that meant giving up some of his time, then so be it.

Bishop stepped into the storage room, pulled a file from a box in the corner, and marched down the aisle to the front door. Everis followed, stopping next to the man as he watched Shar's jeep drive past.

"Our sheriff does make the rounds, doesn't she?" Bishop said.

"She takes her job very seriously. That means she makes herself accessible to her people."

"She isn't so very different than me then." Bishop turned left. "My son is quite infatuated with her."

Everis jerked and shoved down the niggling of jealousy threatening to spring forth. "Really?"

"He admires a beautiful, yet strong woman."

"Sheriff Camenetti isn't one to be as submissive as the other women in your community." He pitied the man who tried to cow her.

"A strong man can bend a woman to his will." Bishop stopped in front of the fire department and faced Everis. "I wasn't sure of his desire to bring her into our fold, but perhaps I was wrong. What do you think, Deputy?"

This might be the chance to get both him and Shar on the inside. "I can talk to her, if you'd like."

"It won't be easy, will it?" Bishop stared into the

distance. "She doesn't seem the type to step down from what should be a man's job and assume her role as a woman. Perhaps, someday, you would be the sheriff of this town. At least until the end of the world as we know it. I can help you with that."

Everis studied the man. Some of his confidence seemed to have slipped, almost as if he were reevaluating plans he thought were cemented in place. "Ending the world or making me sheriff?"

Bishop chuckled. "We need a man with a sense of humor." Without answering, he opened the door to the fire station and entered.

How in the world was Everis going to convince Shar to walk with bowed head and to pretend to have an interest in Bishop's son? Especially if the man was as pretentious as his father?

With a deep sigh, he followed the man into the building.

Chapter Eleven

Shar handed Annie a can of soda, then sat across from her in the interrogation room. She didn't want the girl to feel as if she were under investigation, but this room offered more privacy than her office or the conference room.

Annie popped the tab on her can with a carbonated hiss and tilted the drink to her mouth. She took several gulps before setting the can on the table. "I've missed that."

"How about you start at the beginning and tell me how you got involved with The Church of Superior Essence?" Even with her sheriff mask on, Shar had to struggle not to laugh at the ridiculous name. She pressed the record button on the recorder.

Annie bowed her head. "My parents divorced when I was fifteen."

"Lift your head up, Annie. You aren't at the community. You can look me in the eye when you talk to me."

She slowly raised her head. "My mom remarried.

My stepfather joined the...church shortly after. I was groomed to be one of the elder's wives. His fourth."

Shar raised her eyebrows. "Polygamists?"

"If that means more than one wife, yeah." She took another gulp of her soda. "A woman's sole purpose there is to breed people to populate the new world. The men are selected very carefully so as to be worthy of passing on their bloodline. Not everyone is chosen to do that, so they have other jobs like guarding, or hunting, planting, enforcing."

"Enforcing what?"

Annie swallowed hard. "The rules."

"How?"

The girl visibly shuddered. "Sometimes people disappear, but most of the time they're tied to a post in the middle of the dirt and whipped. Sometimes, they're punished where we don't see. We only hear the screams." She clapped her hands over her ears and folded into herself.

"Annie, look at me." Shar gently pulled the girl's hands away from her head. "You're safe here. No one will hurt you."

"He'll find me. I know he will. He'll find me and he'll kill me."

"He won't kill you. He needs you to make babies." Shar settled back in her seat. If she was right, that would be the primary reason the reverend wasn't interested in Shar. Too old, despite women having babies until forty nowadays. "How old is the oldest woman there?"

"Reverend Bishop's wife is ancient. I'd guess she's at least forty."

Shar rolled her eyes. She'd guess the woman to be

closer to fifty, but unhappiness aged a person. "Are all the babies birthed there, or have some new families brought them along?"

"Some bring them. You have to sign over everything. Your money, whatever belongs to you. It's all for the good of the community." Tears ran down her cheeks. "I have nothing."

"You have the strength and determination to leave a cult. That's big, Annie. Very big. We've had some girls disappear around here. Is the reverend known for bringing in young girls against their will?"

Annie's eyes widened. "Not that I know of, but I wasn't allowed in some buildings."

Shar's cell phone vibrated. She had a text from Everis asking her to join him outside the room. "You relax, Annie. I'll be right back."

She stepped out of the room. "How long have you been here?"

"For the whole session." Everis glanced through the small window in the door. "How do you feel about being courted by Bishop's son?"

"What?" Shar narrowed her eyes.

"It seems the man has a crush on you." Everis grinned.

"Who told you this?"

"Bishop himself. His son is attracted to your beauty and your strength. Seems he wants a woman with a brain to keep him company in his old age."

"I'd rather stick a spoon down my throat, but it's a way to get inside." She watched Annie twirl her can on the table. "I need proof that Bishop's church is a dangerous cult that steals, lies, harms, and possibly murders its members." She met Everis's gaze. "If pretending to be Junior's gal will let me find that proof, then I'm all in."

"You won't be able to stop any of the punishments if you're a witness to them, Shar." His gaze held hers. "Can you stand there and do nothing when a whip is laid across someone's back?"

"I can only promise to try. I won't stand back and let someone be killed."

"Neither will I."

"We need a safe place for Annie."

Everis nodded. "I'll contact someone I know in Little Rock. There's a safe house for young women there. She'll be safe and given the resources to start a new life. Will she testify against Bishop if needed?"

"I think so." Shar reached for the door. "Let me finish up here, and you tell your new best friend that I'd love to meet his son."

Everis stopped her with a hand on the shoulder, then turned her to face him. "Maybe I'll tell Bishop that I'll join only if I can bring you with me. Why should I go along with handing you over like a dove to be sacrificed?"

She smiled. "The best plan I've heard in a long time."

* * *

Bishop's face darkened. His jovial grin faded. "You want me to tell my son that you want the woman he has set his eyes on?"

"I'm sorry, sir. I know we discussed this, but I've cared strongly for Shar since the moment I met her. We have a history together. We can be a powerful couple in your reign." Everis did his best to give Bishop the respect the man thought he deserved and stood ramrod straight, staring at a stain on the wall that looked like the state of California. "I've spoken with Shar in depth…"

"She'll have to change her name."

"Excuse me?" Everis's gaze switched to the man behind the desk.

"We give our women biblical names here. None of this modern, made-up stuff." Bishop steepled his fingers under his chin and gave a smile that chilled Everis to his bones. "Choose carefully. The name you choose will be the name of all the wives you take in the future. The new world will not abide by the rules of the old."

The man was openly admitting to polygamy. "If Shar and I actually decide to join you, I'll name her Sheerah."

"You haven't made your choice?" Bishop's brows rose. "Can you not see the benefits of what we have here? We can be entirely self-sufficient."

Everis held the man's stare. "Why me?" Yes, Everis was good at his job. Yes, he was strong. But that didn't seem enough to warrant the fervent way Bishop tried to convince him to join. "Pardon my questions, but I'm a dark-haired man in a world of blonds. Shar and I will stick out like black roses in a field of white. It's obvious you were aiming for a certain type. What changed?"

"Do you hear the voice of God, Deputy?"

"Perhaps."

"I am merely a mortal man. I hear my God's voice, but only he can see the future. Sometimes plans change to go along with what he sees coming. I've been told that it is more important to have strong people than an army of clones." He pushed to his feet. "Follow me,

Deputy. I'm confident you'll be convinced by the end of our tour. I'm about to show you things others only see after they are baptized."

After the tour, Everis met Shar for a late lunch at their favorite outdoor burger shop. "I'm stunned. There's no other word for the things I saw. The man is definitely missing a rung from his ladder."

Her hand paused on its way to her mouth. A french fry dangled. "Anything illegal?"

"Other than polygamy, which he admitted to in a roundabout way, nothing that I can see yet. The mention of having more than one wife, he said it pertained to the future." Everis shrugged. "There's no laughter in that place, Shar. I only saw the children from a distance. Very well-behaved children. It's creepy."

"Did you see any signs of people being punished?" She popped a fry into her mouth.

"Like Annie was saying?" He shook his head. "There is a post in a courtyard, but no signs that it's used for that purpose."

"Now what?" She licked a bit of ketchup from the corner of her mouth.

Everis focused on her lips. "What?"

"What do we do now?" She grinned.

"I guess your name is now Sheerah—has to be a biblical name—and we go undercover." He forced his gaze away from her lips and how badly he wanted to kiss them. "We'll need to find long-term care for our children." He reached over and laid his hand on top of hers. "Are you sure you want to do this? I have a sinking feeling that what we'll encounter may be worse than Townsend and Smith combined. If Bishop isn't the nice guy he portrays, then he is evil personified."

Her eyes hardened. "If so, I want him out of my town. I'll do whatever it takes to spare other young women like Annie. I know Candy will take care of Robby and Brian."

He stood and held up his hand. "Let's do this."

* * *

"I want her!" Junior glowered across the desk. "I told you that. Why would you let that man have her?"

"She wasn't yours to begin with." The reverend took a sharp breath through his nose. "I want that deputy as one of my elders. If his having the sheriff by his side brings him into the fold, then he may have her."

"Why is this man so important to you? First you use that person to snatch the girls, now you want the deputy."

"You followed the happenings of the last year in Highland Springs. You know this man's dogged determination for justice. I want that in the new world."

"The sheriff was also a part of bringing justice."

"Yes, and she is coming too, just not as your potential wife." The reverend slammed his hands on his desk. "Enough. I've said my piece. Do not question my authority again. You know the consequences."

"I know them well." His son spun and stormed from the room.

The reverend leaned back in his chair. When had things gone from simple to complicated? When he'd met the sheriff and her deputy. When he'd set his sights on a man that would be a great asset in the new world. He could only pray it wouldn't be the biggest mistake he'd ever made.

He left his office and walked the paths of his world.

The sun had just begun its descent, his favorite time of day. Lanterns were lit in the dining hall. The soft clink of eating utensils against porcelain plates rang out.

From between the buildings, a line of children marched single file to their evening meal. The one meal of the day they shared with their parents as a family. Then the families would retire to their individual apartments for recitation before bedtime.

He smiled. He looked forward to the time after supper. Surrounded by his six wives and multiple children. He'd given up the boys in the past, but having accepted his God's new plan for the future, he looked forward to creating more sons to carry on. Sons with his bloodline to mix with the blood of the elders he'd chosen to surround himself with.

He pushed through the door of the dining hall and paused so every head could turn and acknowledge his entrance. Then like the king he was, he headed for the table at the front of the room where his wives were seated.

Junior sat with his own two wives at a table to the reverend's right. He glanced up when the reverend entered, then focused again on the empty plate in front of him.

Once the reverend had taken his seat, the first wives took up their husbands' plates and filled them at the buffet line. Then, the single men filled their plates, followed by the other women and children.

Things ran like clockwork. The reverend couldn't let anything, or anyone, mess that up.

Chapter Twelve

Shar sat on her front porch the next morning and nursed her second cup of coffee. She needed to get up, get dressed, and head to the "community." She wanted to gag every time she said the word.

"It's your fault, you know." Candy, holding a mug of steaming coffee, sat in the rocker next to her.

"What is?" Shar continued to stare across the expanse of lawn in front of her home.

"Caring so much for the people of this town that you would do something so foolishly dangerous in order to keep them safe."

"You don't think I should do this?"

"No, I don't. You have no idea what you're heading into." She put a hand on Shar's arm. "You have a baby and a teenage girl dependent on you. What if something happens to you?"

"Then you and Pinson have a ready-made family." Shar had an inkling of what she was heading into. She trusted her instincts, and Everis seemed to have the same feeling that something was very wrong with The

Church of Superior Essence.

"Don't you need to pack or something?"

"Nope. I can't take anything but the clothes on my back. I do still have a job to do, but I'll be sleeping at the community." She'd keep her gun and clean uniforms at the office. "I can't come back here until this is determined one way or the other." Which broke her heart. No slobbery kisses from Robby or licks from Goliath. She'd even miss the rolling eyes and flouncing off that Mira did on a regular basis. "I wish there was a way to find out whether Bishop is holding people against their will without spending my nights there. Please keep a close eye on Mira. I don't want her disappearing too. I can't be distracted."

"I will. Too bad you can't force his people to talk. What about your Jane Doe?"

"Still in a coma." Shar wasn't holding out much hope in that direction anymore.

Everis pulled into the drive. He climbed out of his car and removed Brian from his car seat before bringing child and seat to the house. The grim expression on his face told Shar all she needed to know about his feelings that morning.

"Good morning. Are you ready?" His voice choked.

"About as ready as you seem to be." Shar stood. "I'm not taking chances. If things get too intense, I'm backing out and calling for help."

"I'm hoping it won't come to that."

"You're holding on to the slim hope he's nothing more than a harmless cult leader?"

"Yes. Until I learn otherwise." He released Brian's hand and set the seat next to the front door. Cupping Shar's face, he said, "I know things are dark there. But I can't worry about you and get to the root of the evil."

She closed her eyes and leaned into his touch. "Don't worry about me. I'll see what I can find out from the women; you do the same with the men. They're so tight-lipped over there it won't be easy." Shar intended to befriend the big man's wife first thing.

She took her mug to the kitchen sink, then turned to say goodbye to Mira and Robby. "Be good, you two. I'll be back as soon as I can."

"If it's a church thing, why can't we come with you?" Mira wiped baby cereal from Robby's chin.

"Because I need to get a feel for the place." Tears stung her eyes as she kissed her son's cheek. "I will miss you so very much, my little man." She straightened and squared her shoulders. "Okay, I'm ready." She grabbed her shoulder holster from the hook by the door and headed for Everis's car.

He soon joined her, and they made the drive to Bishop's place in silence where they were met by the reverend, a younger version of him, and two men armed with rifles.

"Welcome, Deputy, Sheriff." Bishop grinned. "So glad you're considering joining us. I'm sure you'll come to see the light." He motioned to the men who closed in behind Everis and Shar.

Her skin prickled, and she stepped to the side as one of the guards reached for her weapon. "No chance. Not while I'm on duty."

"I'm afraid we must keep our weapons while working, Reverend." Everis glared at the guards.

"Very well, but it goes against our principles to have a woman armed."

Shar slipped her sheriff mask into place. She'd most

likely be wearing the impassive expression twenty-four seven for a while. "I have a job to do. I intend to do it. I'll succumb to your rules when the work day is finished."

He clapped his hands. "Very well. Let me introduce Donald Bishop Junior, my right hand and heir."

Junior held out his hand to Everis, but his gaze landed on Shar. "Pleased to meet you."

Biting the inside of her lip to keep from saying something she shouldn't, she glanced away and focused on Bishop's wife approaching. She moved at a sedate pace, hands clasped around a bundle of tan cloth, head bowed.

She stopped in front of Shar. "Your gowns. One for day, one for night. You'll switch out on laundry day. Please, let me show you to your room."

This was the opportunity Shar had waited for. She hadn't planned on contact so soon, but she wasn't going to pass on it. "Thank you." She cut a quick glance at Everis. "I'll meet you back here in an hour to head to the office."

A muscle ticked in Bishop's jaw. "Please refrain from giving orders while here, Sheriff. I do realize you're the boss, but please put things more in the form of a request, so as not to encourage the women to overstep their boundaries."

For crying out loud. Shar gave a nod and followed Mrs. Bishop to a two-story, wood-frame building.

Mrs. Bishop led her to a room with two beds. "Unfortunately, for propriety's sake, our unwed women share a room. You'll meet your roommate this evening."

"Thank you." Shar flashed a smile. "I hope you and

I will have the opportunity to be friends."

The woman paled. "I am here to teach you our ways. That is all. Supper is served at six p.m. sharp." She backed from the room and scurried away.

Getting her to open up would be a challenge for sure.

* * *

Everis followed Junior to the men's dormitory and was shown to a room with a single bed. Two hooks stuck out from the wall as a place to hang his clothes. A gas lantern rested on a plain, square side table which also held a tin pitcher and bowl with a rag and bar of soap. Primitive indeed.

"As a hopeful privileged member of this community, you are entitled to a private room." Junior drew aside a set of white cotton curtains. "With a view."

Everis stepped to the window and gazed upon the woods behind the community. The room lacked ornamentation, but outside held a scene to soothe any troubled soul. "Thank you."

"I'm to be your teacher. I know you must get to work. Supper is at six. We'll study after." He turned to go.

"Wait." Everis faced him. "I'm sorry for the misunderstanding regarding Sha…Sheerah."

Junior's shoulders stiffened. "May the best man win." His mouth quirked and he left.

The man would seriously make Shar the prize in a challenge? The last thing either Everis or Shar needed was the distraction of a man who thought someone had snatched away the last piece of cake.

With a little over half an hour before he needed to

meet Shar, Everis decided to familiarize himself a bit more with the place. He wandered the halls, noting most of the rooms held two beds. Another building housed small two-bedroom apartments. None had running water or electricity. Bishop was definitely training his people to do without luxuries.

Outside, he retraced his steps from the other day, taking closer note of the location of the chapel, dining hall, and outhouses. He caught a quick glimpse of Shar in the window of the women's dormitory and tossed her a quick wink, then motioned his head toward the gate.

She nodded and let the curtains fall into place. She met up with him at the well. "Anything?"

"Nothing more than that we'll be living in the dark ages at night and on the weekends." He grinned. "And I do believe I've been challenged by Donald Junior."

She raised her eyebrows. "Really?"

"Yep. For you."

"These people are crazy. Do they seriously think the world is ending?"

"I think they have the god complex. It's never occurred to them that people won't see things their way. Look around you." He waved his arm.

"The men do as they're told. The women do as they're told."

"We need to find out what kind of hold Bishop has over them and whether or not the missing girls are here."

* * *

Donald Junior, or DJ as he called himself in private, watched the deputy walk through the gate with the sheriff. She laughed over her shoulder at something he said. DJ's breath caught in his throat. She was the most beautiful woman he'd ever seen.

From the moment he first saw her on the streets of Highland Springs, he'd wanted her. It didn't matter about her age or her mixed family. All he wanted was her. All he saw was her. Now, the very man his father sought threatened to take away the only thing DJ had ever really, truly, wanted.

Since he was the deputy's trainer, he'd make sure the man failed. DJ smiled. The day the man failed and was punished would be one of the few highlights of DJ's life. He wouldn't allow a stranger to waltz into the community and sit at his father's right hand while his only flesh-and-blood son walked the earth.

Chapter Thirteen

Shar was a tee shirt-and-jeans kind of gal with the occasional tank top thrown in during hot weather. In other words, she liked comfort. The rough fabric of the tan shapeless dress she now wore made her regret the undercover assignment more than anything else at the moment. Her skin itched everywhere the cloth touched her skin. She wound her hair on top of her head and secured it with pins. Yep. Dowdy.

"We mustn't be vain," Mrs. Bishop said as she entered the room. "It's a punishable sin. It's time for supper." She turned and left, no doubt expecting Shar to follow without argument.

From sheriff to lamb, all in the space of a day. Shar sighed. Her town was worth the temporary inconvenience.

The first lady, as Shar liked to call her, led Shar to the square, wood building at the end of the compound. "You'll sit with the single women, stand when the reverend enters, and do not speak to any man unless spoken to directly. Then, you speak only what you must. No conversation." A flicker of pain flitted across her face. "Punishment will not only be dealt to you if you disobey. It also falls on me as your trainer."

The last thing Shar wanted to do was cause more pain to the woman already bowed from abuse. Not that she'd witnessed Mrs. Bishop's abuse firsthand, but she recognized the signs. Refusing to make eye contact, a tremor to her hands, a slight stiffening when her husband approached.

Heads turned to stare when they entered the dining hall. Shar gave a quick glance to where Everis sat on the other side of the room, then lowered herself into the chair pointed out to her. She hadn't pulled her chair up to the table before everyone rose to their feet. She stood along with them and watched Bishop take his seat at the front of the room. The man acted like a king. Behind him came his son, then an entourage of women...daughters supposedly. Although Shar was betting her badge they were "wives." Now, she had to prove her theory.

She kept a close eye on the man as he sat and was waited on by Mrs. Bishop. After the men had filled their plates, Shar filed into line with the other women and children. A simple buffet of garden vegetables, ham, and homemade bread made up their meal.

Keeping her head down but her gaze scouring the room, she again resumed her seat. Dinner was a silent affair. Children were quickly hushed. She cast another look at Everis. How did the single mingle in this community if men and women were kept so separate?

Once the meal was finished, the men gone from the room and the tables and dishes cleared, the women and children were then marched to either their private homes or a common room at one end of the apartment building. Shar was instructed to sit in an empty chair across from Mrs. Bishop.

As soon as their leader sat, the women began chanting, "God is good, we are one, what is ours is his, blessed be the name. The end is coming. We are to prepare. We are God's chosen." Repeated so many times that Shar would hear the words in her sleep.

Then, the women pulled baskets from under their chairs and worked on mending and sewing clothes. Shar waited for instructions. When none came, she cleared her throat, then spoke, "Excuse me, but what am I supposed to be doing?"

As if one, all heads snapped toward her. Mrs. Bishop frowned. "You are here to observe. You have not been baptized into the faith, Sheerah. We cannot ask you to work."

She was definitely in an old episode of the *Twilight Zone*. She sighed and pulled at a loose thread on her dress. She would die of boredom before finding out what was going on in this alleged church.

A scream sounded outside.

Shar leaped to her feet and made a dash for the door.

"Sheerah, you mustn't!" Mrs. Bishop rushed toward her. "That is a job for the men."

Shar shook her head. "It's my job as sheriff."

"Not while you're here." The woman tried to grab her arm.

Shar jumped out of reach and ran outside.

The men had congregated on the main path. Everis hurried to Shar's side and took her by the arm. "Get out of sight."

"What's going on?"

"I'm not sure yet, but your being here won't go over well. Please." He cast a glance toward the glowering Bishop. "We have to follow the rules in order to gain their trust."

"Fine. But I expect a full report in the morning." She yanked free and stomped back into the building. Highland Springs's sheriff had been thrust into the background and demoted.

She slipped her impassive mask into place and resumed her seat, shuffling past the wide-eyed Mrs. Bishop. "Don't worry. I've been firmly put in my place in front of all the men in the community." There had to be a way for Shar to sneak out and investigate.

* * *

"You must keep Sheerah under control, Deputy." Bishop paced the path before Everis raced toward the scream.

"I will." He slowed at the tree line and pulled his pistol from its holster. It had taken quite a bit of convincing to get Bishop to allow him to keep his weapon. Two armed guards joined him. Ignoring them, Everis pushed a tree branch out of the way and set off into the darkness.

They found the young girl hiding behind a stand of dried brush.

"Come on out." Everis held out his hand to her. She couldn't be more than fifteen. How many young women tried, and failed, to run away from this place? If not for the guards watching over his shoulder, he would have told the girl to run.

"Don't take me back." Her eyes shimmered with unshed tears in the light of the moon.

He glanced at the guards who stood stony-faced and unmoved by her pleas. "You can't stay out here in the dark. No one is going to hurt you. Why did you scream?"

"I saw a snake." She inched out, and the guards immediately stepped to each side of her, prodding her ahead. Everis stayed a few feet behind and kept his gaze locked on the girl. He meant it when he said no one would harm her.

Bishop waited for them, then led them to his office. "Explain yourself."

The girl stood with her head down. "I don't want to marry Mark."

"You and he are well-suited, and your parents have agreed to the union." Bishop's face darkened. "Don't you want to secure your position in the new world?"

"Yes, sir."

"Put her in confinement until I can think of suitable discipline." He waved a hand at the guards, then turned to Everis. "What would you do in my position?"

"I really don't know. I'm still reeling from the fact that you arrange marriages between virtual strangers." Everis watched the girl and men leave, closing the door behind them.

"With the men and women kept apart, there's no other way to find their spouse, Mr. Hayes. It's an old-fashioned way of doing things, but very effective, and keeps our moral principles in place." He folded his hands on top of his desk. "We opened this community ten years ago and we're growing so fast, we had a need for more land. Hence our coming to your fair town." He grinned. "We've plenty of room to expand, and the neighboring area is rich for the harvest. Young people are too foolish to make wise choices in many things. So for the good of the community, we make them."

"How would you normally punish her, Reverend? Corporal punishment? Humiliation?" Everis squared his shoulders.

The man chuckled. "You act as if I'm a monster."

"Are you?"

His smile dimmed a bit. "Not in the slightest. The community is always my priority." He stood. "The girl will clean all the dishes after each meal for a month. That should give her plenty of time to think about her actions. Is that tame enough for you?"

"Yes." Everis couldn't shake the feeling that his presence had saved the girl from harm, and possibly, death.

"Have a good evening, Mr. Hayes. Tomorrow is Saturday. You'll have plenty of time to familiarize yourself with our community."

"As long as work doesn't call." Everis met the man's hard look and headed back to his room. Catching sight of Shar in the shadows, he switched direction and followed.

* * *

Using the pretense of needing the outhouse, Shar ducked inside the closet-sized building, held her breath against the stench of fifty people, and pulled out the cell phone she'd smuggled into the compound. She checked emails, answered a concern from Mayfield that reporters were converging on the hospital, then turned off the phone and stepped out.

"What are you doing?" Everis stepped from around the corner.

Shar squeaked. "If I'd had my gun, I would have—

why do you have a gun? He let you keep your gun?"

He grinned. "I'm a valuable future member of this community, and a man."

"May I borrow your gun?"

"Why?"

"So I can shoot that grin off your face." She slipped behind the buildings and beckoned for him to follow. "Who screamed?"

"A girl not happy with the man chosen to be her husband." He fell into step beside her. "I got the impression Bishop wasn't happy with the way I thought he should handle the situation."

"You mean he isn't going to whip the girl?"

"He says nothing like that happens as the community is his main concern. I don't believe a word of it, but it's Annie's word against his. I doubt I'll get the opportunity to speak with the latest runaway alone."

"There's no evidence for anything, only suspicion. I'll try to talk to this girl in the evenings." Despair tickled the back of Shar's mind. "Maybe we really are searching where there's nothing to be found."

"I don't think so. They just don't trust us yet." He rested his hands on her shoulders and turned her to face him. "I may have to do something that goes against both of our grains. I may have to skirt the edges of what's legal. Sometimes, undercover work asks us to do what we wouldn't normally do."

"Like what?" She searched through the night for his eyes. If she could look into them, she'd be secure in knowing that nothing Bishop had said had convinced Everis to turn to their way of thinking. He couldn't consider such a thing, could he?

"Anything that doesn't require someone dying." He

released her. "Will you stand back and let me do what needs doing?"

"I can't promise that I will stay here. If I don't find something fast to warrant staying, I'll go back to the town I'm hired to protect."

"I understand. It might be better for you to return home and let me handle things here anyway."

"No. Unless something happens that tears at my conscience, you need me to watch your back for as long as possible." As she needed him to watch hers.

The sound of a footfall on the other side of the building plastered them against the wall. Shar's heart thudded so loud she thought those sleeping inside would wake. She relaxed when no one appeared around the corner.

"Let's do some snooping." She took Everis by the hand. "Tell me about the men's dormitory."

"A common room, a few single beds, mostly rooms with double beds."

"No different than the women, then." They wouldn't find anything within the walls of the buildings. "We need to find someone here that will talk. Mrs. Bishop is little more than a frightened mouse."

"Other than Junior's challenge, I've not spoken to anyone but Bishop since I arrived."

They stopped at the edge of the dining hall. "How are we supposed to know whether or not we want to join if no one will talk to us?"

"A training or something?"

"Like a seminar?"

"Maybe. Bishop did say I'd have more time, since tomorrow was Saturday. The man seems to think crime only runs nine-to-five on weekdays. He wasn't happy when I told him we'd have to leave if something came up."

"At least he let you keep your cell phone. I had to sneak mine in. Speaking of..." she peered around the corner. "Mayfield said reporters have gathered at the hospital. Our Jane Doe may be waking up."

"That's good news."

Shar started to respond with "yes, it was" when Everis pulled her close, wrapped his hands in her hair, and kissed her. Her breath left her in a gasp. It wasn't until someone coughed that he released her.

Bishop and his son glared from the corner of the building. "There seems to be some kind of misunderstanding," Bishop said.

Everis moved slightly in front of Shar. "Just trying to grab some alone-time with my girl."

"At the risk of her reputation." He shook his head. "I'm aware you aren't completely familiar with the way we do things. I'll do my best to be patient with you, but I think we need to step up your training. Both of you, meet me in the dining hall immediately after breakfast." He stormed away, back straight.

Junior leaned close to Shar. "I will come courting tomorrow evening. Something we do not do here, but my father said he will make an exception in this case. Good night, Mr. Hayes." He followed his father.

Shar wrinkled her nose. "Is liquor allowed here?"

"I've never asked. The man did reek of whiskey when he talked though."

Bishop glared around the building. "Back to your rooms, please. Do not make me ask again."

"Or what?" Shar mumbled. "He asks as if we've already joined him."

"He isn't used to taking no for an answer." Everis took her hand in his. "Kissing you was the quickest thing I could think of as an excuse to be caught out after curfew."

She smiled up at him. "I'm not adverse to a goodnight kiss."

He lowered his head and obliged.

* * *

Bishop stared out his window as the deputy kissed the sheriff again, despite his orders. The man might not be worth the trouble of conversion after all. He also had his doubts about the sheriff. Too beautiful and headstrong to ever be submissive to anyone.

Doubts rose in his chest. Those two were up to something, and it wouldn't bode well for The Church of Superior Essence. Especially if Rachel woke from her coma.

He turned away from the window. Desperate times were coming. Times that would test his faith and strength. His very obedience. He could not let anyone stand in his way of fulfilling his destiny.

Not even his son.

Chapter Fourteen

A commotion at the front gate led Everis away from the path to the dining hall and to a red-faced, arm-waving, curse-spewing Pinson. "Hey. What's up?" He motioned for the guards to step back.

Shar, fully dressed in her uniform, rushed to his side. "I saw Pinson from my window."

Pinson opened his mouth, then snapped it closed. Taking a deep breath, he started over. "We've a situation the sheriff needs to handle. I don't want to talk about it in front of...civilians. Especially ones too stupid to cooperate with law enforcement."

Everis chuckled, knowing Pinson had to dig deep to find something nice to call the stony-faced guards. "We're coming." He turned to Tweedle Dee and Tweedle Dum, his new names for the guards, and asked that they let the reverend know duty called him and the sheriff away for a while, and that they'd attend the orientation later.

Side by side, he walked with Shar to where he'd left his car just outside the gate. Once out of earshot of those watching from the gate, he turned to Pinson. "I'm listening."

"Someone knocked Mayfield over the head sometime early this morning and slit Jane Doe's throat. I closed off that floor of the hospital and told the doctors that nobody leaves. But with you two here, Mayfield down, the agents following a hunch in the southern part of the state...I can't guarantee the security of the scene."

Everis closed his eyes and took a moment to compose himself. "Is Mayfield all right?"

"Other than a concussion, yes. I'll follow the two of you to the hospital."

"Someone at the hospital is working with Bishop." Shar climbed into the car and slammed her door closed. "Which doesn't fit with the little we do know. No one works outside the compound."

"Maybe they made an exception in this case or there is someone like us that hasn't made their final decision." Everis sped toward the hospital. "Don't forget our phantom abductor."

"Do you think there's an initiation of sorts?"

"Maybe." They couldn't rule out anything.

"We've not heard anything on the high school interviews or shoe comparison either. We're dealing with a very smart suspect."

Mayfield sat in a curtained-off room when they arrived. He looked up with a sheepish expression. "Sorry, Sheriff... I stepped into the room to use the restroom, and someone conked me while doing my business. I woke up to a nurse screaming and machines beeping. A man don't like getting caught with his pants down."

Everis shot a quick glance at a wide-eyed Shar. Under different circumstances, the moment would be funny. As it was, it was tragic. "Since you're going to survive, I'm headed to the victim's room."

"I've never run up against such an impregnable wall before," Shar said. "This suspect is good. Maybe better than me."

"Nobody is better than you." He glanced over. "Trust your gut. You're always watching, always listening. You can do this."

"Always the encourager."

He'd let the poison darts of doubt prick him before and almost fallen so far he thought he'd never recover. By encouraging Shar, he kept his own hopes up. They *would* catch the person responsible for Jane Doe's and her baby's death. They would lock up the person responsible for the missing girls.

He stood next to the hospital bed and stared at a pretty face the same color as the sheets were before stained with blood. Who are you? The things you could have told us. "We need to talk to Annie again."

"I agree." Shar stepped away and asked Pinson to call the agents to bring her back from Little Rock. "Annie must know a way to tip Bishop's hand. Let's split up and question those on this floor. I'll take the east wing. Maybe Agent Mills and Agent Rollins can pick up Annie."

Everis took one last look at the girl whose life had been cut too short, then went to find a doctor he could trust to help corral the staff and patients. The head resident was more than willing and set Everis up in an empty waiting room.

"I'll send them in one by one and try to find out

whether anyone left the floor after the…murder." The man paled. "These things don't happen here."

"They just did." Everis took his seat. "I appreciate the help." Everis set a small tape recorder he kept in his pocket on the table and waited.

The first person to enter the room was an older nurse. With her thin shoulders squared, she stepped in and took the seat across from him. "I'm Nurse Betty. Well, Betty Lincoln. Jane Doe was my patient. Mine to care for. I couldn't feel worse about what happened."

"It isn't your fault, Ms. Lincoln. We're dealing with very bad, incredibly crafty people. Did you see anyone who wasn't a regular on the floor? Anyone you didn't know?"

＊
＊　＊

After the third teary-eyed but clueless nurse, Shar was ready to throw her hands up. Not that she wasn't empathetic with their feelings of being so close to murder, but the eleventh hour hovered over her head before she had no reason to continue pursuing Bishop on a hunch. They needed more than a gut feeling. They needed proof.

With Jane Doe in a coma, she hadn't required a lot of checking on, just routine monitoring. One day nurse and one night nurse handled what needed to be done. The others knew only what the assigned nurses told them.

That left non-medical personnel, visitors, and patients. Shar pushed up from the table in the small lounge she'd taken over and headed to a room. Door to door was an old-fashioned way of doing things, but often the most effective.

She knocked on the first door. "Sheriff Camenetti,

may I come in?"

A feeble voice called for her to enter. "It's nice to finally meet you."

Shar glanced at the white board on the wall. "Henrietta…"

"Jones, but you call me Henrietta." The elderly woman gave a toothless grin. "Sit. I'm sure you're here about the murder."

Shar narrowed her eyes, but sat in the chair beside the bed. "What do you know about that?"

Henrietta tapped a gnarled finger on her temple. "I see things and I hear things. I don't sleep well, and I tend to wander the floor at night."

"You saw something?"

"I'm not quite sure. Last night was a bit strange, if truth be told. Nurse Betty went in and out a few more times than what seemed normal. I've got a clear line of sight from here to that room."

Shar glanced over her shoulder. She could see the foot of Jane Doe's bed. She smiled. "I think you might be my new best friend."

"If only, sweetie." She patted Shar's hand. "The weird thing about last night and Nurse Betty is…her walk changed. Nurse Betty is a little bird of a woman who carries herself like an amazon. Full of confidence that one. But sometimes last night, she seemed hesitant and unsure of herself."

Shar sent a quick text to Everis to join her in room 111 and to bring along Nurse Betty. "I cannot tell you how much I appreciate you being a nosy person, Henrietta," Shar said. "You may have given us our first real clue in all this."

"Wouldn't that be something?" Her eyes twinkled.

"My final good act before this cancer takes me."

A twinge of regret pierced Shar's heart. "I would have liked to have known you better." She felt as if she and the old woman could have been very close indeed.

"Well, I might have a few more months in me, who knows? There's a handsome man standing in the doorway."

Shar glanced over her shoulder. "That's one of my deputies. Deputy Hayes, meet Henrietta Jones."

Everis stepped forward, took the woman's wrinkled hand in his and raised it to his lips. "My pleasure."

"Mercy, young man. You'll give me a heart attack acting like that. Where's the nurse?" Her cheeks reddened.

"I'm here, Miss Henrietta." A woman very much like the description given bustled into the room.

This was not a hesitant woman by any means. Shar stood. "I'm Sheriff Camenetti. Do you have a few minutes?"

"I have all the time you need. I'm pulling a double shift."

"Wonderful. How many times did you visit Jane Doe last night?"

"Once an hour on the hour as always."

Shar flicked a glance at Henrietta. "Different?"

"The two o'clock visit. You—or someone pretending to be you—entered that room before two-thirty." Henrietta crossed her thin arms. "Nothing wrong with my eyesight."

"It takes me five to ten minutes to check a patient's vitals. If someone came in by two-fifteen or later, it wasn't me." Nurse Betty stepped next to Henrietta's bed. "Do you need anything while I'm here?"

"Not a thing, nurse, thank you." Henrietta smiled, then focused back on Shar. "Well? What now?"

"We go catch a killer." Shar motioned her head toward the door. "Deputy?"

"Meet you out there." Everis marched from the room.

"I'll be back to visit you, Henrietta. I promise." Shar placed a hand on the woman's bony shoulder and gave a gentle squeeze. "Don't go dying on me."

"Not today." Henrietta grinned and waved her on. "Go do your job."

Shar laughed and joined Everis in the hall. "We're looking for a small woman the size of Nurse Betty in a sea of women wearing scrubs. That's if the woman was on the staff at the hospital and not someone who entered solely for the purpose of murder."

"I'm thinking the second statement might be accurate. It can't be that easy."

She frowned. "It wouldn't be easy if she was on staff here. They come and go like a revolving door."

"Then we line them up like cattle about to be branded and mark them off a list." Everis approached a man in his early forties, spoke a few words, then returned with a clipboard. "We're starting with the day crew, including cafeteria staff. We'll be here until morning."

She shrugged. "Darn. We'll miss orientation."

* * *

"It's finished." Junior stood rigid in front of the reverend's desk. "Rachel is dead and so is the woman who did the job for us."

The Reverend smiled, rubbing his hands together. "Wonderful. We'll use her disobedience, as we'll tell everyone, to convince the others of the importance of doing what they are told. Her husband will either turn over his other bank account or lose his son as well. We cannot sufficiently provide for our future without funds to purchase certain things."

"May I speak frankly, sir?"

"Of course." The reverend motioned for him to have a seat.

His son sat, then met his father's gaze. "It seems as if we're losing more of our congregation than we're having join us."

"We're culling out the weak. We need a handful of strong men, twice that many women, and we'll grow our own population. We've several we need only to convince. Until then, they are safe in the hole." He leaned back in his chair, causing the worn leather to creak. "Sometimes I feel as if you're losing sight of our vision. Instead of questioning me, you should be choosing another wife, now that Rachel is gone."

"I have my eye on someone."

"The sheriff."

"Not the sheriff. She isn't to have children with unless our god grants it in our older age. I want the girl promised to Mark. She has spunk. I like that. I enjoy molding the younger wives into perfect submission."

The reverend laughed. "Perhaps you've got what it takes to follow in my footsteps after all. You may have her and one of the girls, as well. We will have the ceremony between you and the feisty one following church tomorrow."

Junior stood. "Thank you. The others are waiting for our evening time. I will see you in the morning." He headed for the door, then stopped, his hand on the doorknob. "The sheriff and deputy missed their orientation. Perhaps they aren't worthy of us after all."

"They missed because of Rachel's death. Something that needed doing. I could care less about the sheriff, Donald, but I want men of the deputy's strength. If I could get Hayes and Pinson to both join us, we'd be that much stronger. When the end comes, the unbelievers will converge on us wanting to take what is ours. We need to be able to show force."

Junior faced him. "I wasn't aware you wanted the older deputy."

"Men can still breed well into their advanced age. Pinson has proven his strength in coming back after his recent gunshot injury."

Junior nodded. "Anything else?"

"Find someone new to pilfer medication from the hospital. The world is coming to an end quickly. I feel it."

Chapter Fifteen

Shar stared at a projector screen and watched as a red-faced Bishop tried to convince anyone watching about the upcoming end of the world. He stressed how important it was to survive as one entity, coming together as a whole. According to Bishop survival meant being led by a shepherd who knew the risks and could handle the trials. The video showed natural disasters, people starving in third-world countries, and wars.

Shar understood being prepared for hard times. She'd suffered enough of those during her thirty-eight years, but to try and convince people with fear...it didn't sit well with her. Trying not to be conspicuous, she cut a sideways glance to where Everis sat on the other side of the room. Other than Bishop and his guards, they were the only two people there. Everis didn't look any more impressed than Shar did.

Once the video finished, Bishop moved to the front of the room. He gave his big grin and clasped his hands in front of him. "I'm sure you can see why we are so convinced it is up to us to keep mankind moving forward. This is why we seek out and approach strong men and women in their child-bearing years. When the end comes, those who are unprepared will perish. Surely you see the wisdom in joining The Church of Superior Essence."

"Not me." Shar stood, shot an apologetic glance to Everis, then stepped into the aisle. "I don't agree with multiple wives, corporal punishment, or kidnapping."

He frowned. "None of that is happening here."

"I know for a fact you practice polygamy. I don't have proof of any of the other accusations, but I'm pretty sure I'm correct. Sorry, Everis, but I cannot find those missing girls by sitting here listening to this nonsense." She turned and stomped from the building.

Everis raced after her and spun her to face him. "What are you doing? I thought we were in this together."

"We are, but I can't make it look as if I'm an easy convert. It would be completely against my character. Besides, I think Bishop suspects something." She headed for the gate.

"Why do you think that?" He caught up with her and fell into step beside her.

"A feeling when he looks at me." She glanced over Everis's shoulder to where Bishop watched from the front of the chapel and shuddered. "With girls disappearing and hospital staff found dead in supply closets, one of us needs to be here, the other out there."

"He'll never believe my story without you. We need to at least spend our nights here. Can you do that?"

She glanced into his eyes, lost in their softness. "How will you explain my temper tantrum?"

He grinned, sending her heart into flips. "Just as you said. You're a stubborn wench who needs to be taught a lesson."

She tilted her head. "Really?"

"Nah, I'm going to tell him you are so committed to your job that your work ethic won't allow you to relax for even a minute, and that I'll continue to convince you." He gripped her shoulders and gave her a shake. "Just for emphasis. Now look properly humbled while I go talk to Bishop."

From Bishop's posture, Shar got the impression he didn't fully believe Everis's story, but then his shoulders relaxed and he glanced her way. Good. Somehow, Everis had sweet-talked the man, same as he did everyone else, and convinced him of their story. A few minutes later, Everis returned.

"He's agreed that for now, your job is important. I agreed to run for sheriff at the next election." He grinned. "Then, you won't feel the need to spend your days working and can become a wife as God intended."

"Good grief." She stormed out the gate and to her jeep. "Can we stop and see the children?"

"Sounds wonderful to me." He slid in the passenger side. "I miss my boy."

"I need fifteen minutes to be nothing but a mom. That's all. Then I'll head over to the high school and talk to some boys. Maybe I'll pick up on something the agents missed." The stress of missing girls and trying to determine whether Bishop was the leader of a cult that may have kidnapped the girls left Shar wrung out and empty. Baby kisses would be just the medicine to cure what ails her. Then, she could focus. "I give Bishop my evenings. During the days and on weekends, I'm still the sheriff."

"Agreed." He took her hand and gave a gentle squeeze. "I know it's hard for you to be cooped up. You're like a beautiful blackbird that needs room to fly. We'll bring down whoever is behind the abductions, find out what Bishop is up to, then get back to our boring lives."

"If only they were boring. This town hasn't settled down since Lars Townsend." She started to believe it would never again be the friendly town she once knew.

Since the sheriff had her little gangsta girl locked up tight and guarded by the sheriff's sister and giant dog, The Man ventured out of town to find his next lucky gal. Once the girls understood the importance of what the community was doing, they'd realize how lucky they were.

He watched as a yellow-haired girl of sixteen or so, sweet and as wholesome-looking as any Midwestern girl, carried a bucket to the barn. From the way she swung her arms, he figured the bucket was empty. It would be easy to grab her within the recesses of the building.

Once she stepped inside, he skirted around to the back, and froze when a dog barked from the other side of the wood wall. When the barking didn't stop, a small door on the side of the barn opened.

The girl peered around the edge. "Hello? Hush, Boomer."

"Yeah, uh, hi. I'm lost and was wondering…"

Her eyes narrowed in suspicion. She might be country, but he could see she wasn't stupid. Maybe he'd take her and Carol both as wives. "Just point the way to the road…"

"There aren't any hiking trails around here. You're on private property. I suggest you leave before my daddy shoots you." She slammed the door closed, effectively halting any way of him taking her.

"Sorry to bother you." He spun and raced back to the van. There were other farm girls to be had. Not all of them were as suspicious as she.

A few miles down the road, he spotted a girl riding a horse and leading another toward a large red barn. The Man turned onto a dirt road just past the barn and waited until she dismounted and led both animals into the building. Not seeing a dog anywhere close by, and the house being at least a football-field length away, he slipped in the back door and pulled his Tazor from his pocket.

She hummed as she brushed the horse. The Man smiled and crept up behind her. If not for the horse nickering, she would never have known he was there. As it was, she turned, eyes wide.

"Hello," he said, pressing the button on the Taser.

She fell into his arms.

* * *

"Got a man on line one that said someone tried to take his daughter." Amber popped her gum, then retreated from the doorway of the conference room.

Shar grabbed the phone. "Sheriff Camenetti."

"Yeah, my girl said some guy was sneaking around our barn. If she hadn't had the dog with her, there's no telling what might have happened."

Shar grabbed a pen and notepad from the center of the table. "What's your name, sir?"

"Ed Roaring. My girl's name is Sue."

"Could the two of you come in and give us a description of this guy?" This might be their big break.

"You bet." Click.

"Got another on line two." Amber toasted them with a coffee mug on her way past.

Shar met Everis's worried gaze, then pressed line two. "Sheriff Camenetti."

"My daughter is gone." A woman's shrill voice pierced Shar's eardrum. "She was riding her horse. The horse is in the barn, the brush is in the hay, and my Ashley isn't here."

"What's your name and address?" Shar scribbled it down. "We'll be right there." She hung up and stood. "We either have an injury or a missing girl. Let's go."

Everis raced outside to the jeep with her. "At this point, I'm hoping injury."

"Strange as it is, me too." If this girl had been abducted, the person responsible was getting very brave. While Shar had noticed the absence of young teen girls on the streets of town, this girl was at home. Same as the one coming in to give a description. "If this person is risking detection by snatching girls from their yards, he really doesn't expect to get caught."

"He will," Everis said. "Coming out in the open like that, at people's homes, increases the risk of being seen. We might have gotten lucky enough to finally know what he looks like."

"I sure hope so. Interviewing the boys at the school didn't result in anything." Other than frustration anyway. No one knew a thing. No one had seen anything. This girl coming into the office was their only hope at this point.

"Chasing this guy cuts into our investigation of

Bishop." Everis shook his head. "I know the man is breaking the law. Maybe in more than one way. Extortion, polygamy, abuse. You name it and I bet he's into it."

"I agree and if we're right, we'll be locking him up for a long time. Right now, we have to find these girls. Preferably alive." She turned onto the highway. "Someone killed Jane Doe, no one has reported her missing, we haven't received any more cut-off fingers or other body parts, we have nothing to tie Bishop to any of this, other than a gut feeling and the fact Jane Doe was wearing a nightgown similar to Annie's dress. Plain."

"Don't forget the girl I found in the woods. She wore something similar." He took her hand. "Bishop is involved. We'll prove it."

"Do you think the missing girls are hidden somewhere in his community?" Shar mentally ran through all the buildings in her mind. "Where?"

"We'll have to look harder."

"Virtually impossible with those two guards roaming around night and day."

"They aren't there twenty-four seven. In the very early hours, the guards are men in their early twenties who jump at shadows." He chuckled. "I know because I suggested to Bishop that his regular guards needed at least four hours of sleep a night."

Shar grinned. "You are a smart man, Deputy Hayes." All they had to do now was sneak out in the middle of the night and snoop around without getting caught. Sounded easy, but she knew it would be far from   that.

Chapter Sixteen

Shar stared out the window at the two-story, white clapboard farmhouse. A massive magnolia tree shaded the wraparound porch. An idyllic setting marred by evil. "Any word on who the dead woman in the hospital is?"

It hadn't surprised her a bit to hear a woman the size of Nurse Betty had been found with her throat slit in a supply closet of the hospital the morning after Jane Doe's death. This whole case was full of holes and went in every direction but straight.

"Not yet. Pinson said he asked for a rush on the prints." Everis shoved open the passenger side door of the jeep. "Ready?"

"Yes." She exited the jeep and headed for the house. Her heart sat heavy. There was only one thing worse than interviewing parents of a missing child, and that was telling them their child was dead. Shar could only hope and pray she didn't have to tell the parents of the missing girls they'd found their daughters' bodies.

A woman darted out the front door and down the

steps before Shar and Everis reached the house. She grabbed Shar's hands. "Find my Ashley."

Shar cleared her throat against the tears clogging it. "Can you show us where she was last?"

After releasing Shar's hands, Mrs. Worthen led them to the barn. "My husband is at a farmer's convention in Oklahoma. I called him right before calling you and he's on his way. He's very distraught." She showed them into the barn. "Her horse is here. I haven't touched a thing. She would never have let Maple Bun unattended like this or left the grooming brush in the dirt."

Shar made note of the drag marks in the dirt aisle between the stables and motioned silently to Everis. To give him the opportunity to investigate without an anxious mother hovering, Shar led the woman out the front and around to the back where a pasture gate hung open. "Is this where she was riding?"

"Yes."

Shar's gaze drifted across the expanse of green to a line of trees at the other end. "Is that a road?"

"A dirt road we use to haul hay."

If the perp parked on the road, then carried Ashley, he had to be a strong man. He wouldn't have dragged her that far—too slow. "I'd like to see Ashley's room." Not that she expected to find anything, but she could never rule out the possibility of the girl leaving on her own.

While Everis scanned the barn for clues, Shar followed Mrs. Worthen to a second-floor bedroom. A four-poster bed took up most of the room and was covered with a crazy quilt. A white desk held a closed laptop. A red tee shirt stuck out of a half-closed dresser drawer. A closet door stood open. A backpack sat next to the desk. Otherwise, the room was tidy. Nothing suggested the girl had run away from home.

"I'd like a list of names and phone numbers to Ashley's friends, please." Shar stepped up to the window and gazed down at the pasture. If only someone had stood here when Ashley had been carried away.

"Here you go." Mrs. Worthen handed Shar a small bright-pink address book. "Ashley has a cell phone, but she likes to write things down."

"Which might help us." Shar took a deep breath. "We'll keep you informed of our investigation. Please call us if you hear from Ashely."

Tears welled in the woman's eyes. "That fiend has her, doesn't he? Just like those other girls."

"We don't know that. Please don't lose hope." Shar would do well to remember her own words.

* * *

"Get me the sheriff's live-in girl." The reverend slammed his hand on the top of his desk. "If I have her, I can convince the sheriff, which in turn will make Deputy Hayes more willing to join. What happens to the sheriff and the girl once we have Hayes does not concern me."

The idiot boy stared as if he didn't have any sense in his head. "She doesn't leave the house since I tried to get her once already. I've brought you four others and can get you more, but she's going to be tough. Plus, there's that giant dog of hers."

"Wait for an opportunity and stop giving me excuses. Get the baby too." The reverend grinned. "And the agent's boy." That ought to bring them running. If the sheriff and deputy didn't stop playing games, he'd decide against bringing them into the fold and simply dispose of them, thus freeing the sheriff position for one of his own. Perhaps himself. Yes, that idea definitely had merit.

"I'll see what I can do." The young man backed from the office.

If he couldn't do it, then the reverend would find someone who could. He sat in his chair, the leather squeaking under him. Junior had a good point. Why was he so set on bringing the agent in? The world was full of strong men.

Was it because the man was well-respected in the community and would, by association, raise Reverend Bishop's reputation in the eyes of the town? If so, wouldn't it be best to focus more on the sheriff who was well-loved?

Perhaps some time spent in the chapel would soothe him and allow him to hear from god. He pushed to his feet and strolled between the dormitories to the simple structure at the end.

Sunlight streamed through windows kept spotless. Since he held services in town, the chapel was rarely used. Someday, this would become the only place to worship. His feet thudded on the wooden floors as he made his way to the kneeling pads at the front, the only bit of luxury allowed in the building.

He knelt, bowed his head, and waited.

* * *

Everis snapped photos of the drag marks on the floor of the barn. It didn't take a forensic scientist to know someone had been dragged. The marks looked exactly like what they were, two evenly-spaced boot heels consistent with what a person would wear riding a horse.

He followed the tracks out the back door. They disappeared in the grass of the pasture, but his bet was that the perp had picked up Ashley Worthen and carried her to his vehicle. Everis jogged to the dirt road on the other side of the pasture and studied the tire tracks. They looked the same as the ones at the scene where the first two girls disappeared.

He phoned Agent Mills and asked that an alert be put out for any suspicious vans and for them to set up a press conference. It was time to alert the people that it wasn't only in town that the danger existed. It was there in their own backyard.

Walking back along the path he'd taken across the pasture, he spotted Shar waiting next to the jeep. She leaned against the hood, her long legs crossed in front of her. He was once again struck by her beauty. Not just the outside, but inside as well. She really, truly loved the people of Highland Springs. Their pain was her pain, and he could see it in every line of her body.

She glanced up as he approached. "Find out anything?"

"Just that the suspect probably carried her to a van and left via that dirt road." He stopped in front of her. "You?"

"Nothing to indicate that she left willingly." She pushed away from the jeep and headed for the driver's side door. "It appears that she's another victim." She lifted a tortured gaze to him. "Where are these girls?"

"We'll find them." He was as tired of his automatic reassurances as Shar was. "I don't know if we'll find them. We'll try."

"Thank you for being honest." She climbed into the jeep and started the engine.

Upon their return, Amber wasted no time in letting them know that a father and daughter waited for them in the conference room, and they were growing impatient. "I told them you were on another call, but you know how some people are." She turned back to her monitor.

"I'll let you handle this one," Shar told him. "I think I'd like to sit back and observe. Maybe I'll pick up on something I've missed."

He nodded and opened the conference room door. "Thank you for coming, Mr. Roaring, Miss Roaring. Have you spoken to our artist?"

"Nobody has showed up here but your receptionist." Mr. Roaring glared and crossed his arms. "My daughter has been traumatized, and we've been kept waiting."

Shar sat across from him. "I'm sorry for the inconvenience, sir, but your daughter is very lucky. The girl whose home we came from isn't."

Spots of color appeared on his cheeks. "I'm sorry, Sheriff. These abductions have to stop."

"Yes, sir, they do."

"If we may." Everis set a tape recorder on the table. "Sheriff, if you could get Mayfield in here to draw this perp, we could send the picture to every news station in the state."

Shar nodded and typed into her phone.

Everis directed his attention back to the man and girl. "Any objections to my taping this interview?" When they shook their heads no, he continued, "Please state your names, then Sue, if you could tell us what happened this morning, we can move forward."

"I was feeding my horse when my dog started barking. He wouldn't stop, so I knew someone was outside of the barn. What made me suspicious was that they weren't at the front door, but the back." She tilted her head. "A visitor would come to the front, right?"

"Most likely."

"So I opened the back door, just enough to look out and saw a guy standing there."

"Can you describe him?"

"He was about your height and wore a blue baseball cap pulled down low over his face. He had a kind of square chin, I think. I couldn't see but half of his face and he kept turning away from me. He talked friendly, but turning away from me made me think he was up to no good."

Her father patted her hand. "Sue is a real smart girl."

"I remembered those girls disappearing and didn't want to be one of them. So I told him to go away and closed the door." She stared at her lap and sighed. "I know who it is. At least, I think I know. I've seen him at school." She looked up. "Do you have a yearbook?"

Everis grinned. "No, but we can get one."

"Already on it," Shar said. "I'll have Mayfield grab one from the school on his way in."

Ten minutes later, Sue flipped through a yearbook. She turned a page, then went to the one before, then back to the next. "I'm pretty sure this is him."

Shar glanced at the page. "Let's go bring Scott Baker in."

CYNTHIA HICKEY

Chapter Seventeen

"Our son hasn't been home in over a week," Mrs. Baker said. Her eyes flashed. "That boy suddenly thinks he's too big for his britches, so he left. Said he was going to make it on his own."

Shar stared at the woman in disbelief. Could it be possible that the friendly young man they'd spoken with a few days ago was the abductor? She'd looked into his eyes, spoken with him. "Any idea where he is now?"

"I've seen him around town, but no idea where he's staying."

"I'll put out an APB," Everis said, stepping off the porch.

"If you see your son, please have him call us." Shar handed the woman a business card. "Does he go to church by chance?"

"No idea." The woman crossed her arms. "Good luck. He isn't the same child I raised."

"Thank you for your time." Shar joined Everis by the jeep. "I don't believe in coincidences."

"Neither do I." Everis put his phone in his pocket. "I think when we find Scott Baker, we'll find our abductor."

The thought made Shar nauseous. What would compel a good-looking high school senior to abduct girls? And if he was the perp, where was he hiding them?

She climbed in the jeep and drove back to the office. Instead of exiting the vehicle, she turned to Everis. "Did you see anyone close to Scott Baker's age at Bishop's compound?"

"No, but that doesn't mean anything. What are you thinking?"

"What if Scott takes the girls there to be brainwashed into the church?"

"We did mention trying to find a possible location."

She nodded and stared at the reporters converging on the sheriff office steps. She'd forgotten the press conference. "Everything seems to lead there, but we have no evidence. Do you want to stake out Baker's house tonight or the compound?"

"Let's do Baker's house and have Mayfield and Pinson do the compound. If nothing happens, we'll switch tomorrow night."

"It's a plan." She exited the jeep and approached the reporters.

The piranhas attacked. "Do you have a suspect?"

"Are you going to enforce a curfew?"

"Will you be getting more help from Little Rock?"

Shar held up her hands to quiet the fray. "We will be enforcing a curfew. At nightfall, we will not allow any person under the age of eighteen to be out. We have two agents at our disposal who are going door-to-door investigating. Someone here in Highland Springs knows where these girls are and who is taking them." She squared her shoulders and stared into the camera. "We do have a suspect, and I'd like to direct my next comment to him. We're coming and we're taking the girls back." She stepped back and entered the building.

"You really don't like the cameras, do you?" Everis asked following her.

"Nope. It's a necessary evil of the job." She headed straight for her office and typed Scott Baker's name into the search engine.

His social media went from fun-loving high school football player to a young man teetering on the edge of obsession. "Everis, come look at this." She pointed to his latest post from three days ago. "Prepare, the end is coming. Only the worthy will survive."

"That sounds a lot like the garbage Bishop spouts." He put a hand on her shoulder. "Let's go pay the reverend a visit."

As suspected, the man denied knowing Scott. "I've never seen that young man in my life. Why would I ask someone who is little more than a child to steal women for me?"

"Why not?" Shar motioned toward the door to her left. "Mind if we step through there?"

"I do mind. That is for my private use."

"We can get a warrant."

Everis stepped forward. "Please pardon the sheriff. She's quite…tenacious." He cut her a warning look.

Shar pressed her lips together. It was difficult to remember that to get any information from Bishop, she had to be meek and submissive. She turned as the door behind her opened.

Donald Bishop, Jr. entered, his gaze landing on Shar. "I'd still like that date, Sheriff."

She forced a smile. "Perhaps when things settle down."

"We shouldn't wait too long. We might not be here." He transferred his attention to his father. "We've something that needs your attention."

"Duty calls." Bishop stood. "I'm sure you understand, right, Sheriff?"

"May we tag along? If we're to make a decision regarding joining you, it's imperative we see all aspects of your operation."

Junior gave a subtle shake of his head. "I'm afraid this is of a...personal nature. Next time, maybe."

"We'll return at a more convenient time." Shar's smile faded the moment she and Everis stepped out of the gate. "I'm sorry I fail at playing the submissive role."

He laughed. "You can't change who you are, and acting is obviously not one of your many talents. We'll be back when they least expect us."

"Do you think he's lying about knowing Scott Baker?"

"Oh, yeah."

"Me too."

The reverend followed his son to the underground bunker where the new girls were stored. He stood in the doorway, his mouth watering at the sight of the four nubile faces. But not one of them was ready to be inducted into the community, and with the sheriff and deputy still not convinced of the community's importance, they couldn't be trained properly.

"What's the problem?" He glanced at his son. "They seem healthy enough."

"One of them says she's pregnant."

"I am." One of the brunettes stood up. "I have a doctor's appointment tomorrow."

"That's wonderful news." The Reverend clapped his hand. "Not only are we saving your life by bringing you here, but your baby's. We have a midwife who is sufficient for your needs."

"I'm not keeping it."

He stared at her as his blood ran hot. "You are now." He stormed from the room and slammed the door. "Make sure she doesn't do anything stupid, Junior. Put her in a room by herself with nothing but a mattress on the floor. What she carries is precious."

"Yes, sir."

"And find someone to break her rebellious spirit."

"I'd love to."

The Reverend returned to his office and through the door the sheriff had been curious about. The cement floor had been scrubbed clean after the last whipping, but a close look would reveal the room for what it was. A chamber of discipline. The room needed modifying to look more like storage. Discipline would have to take place underground.

He closed the door and stepped outside. His gaze roamed across his land to the gate. Things had become too complicated. He no longer cared whether the sheriff and deputy joined him. He would play their game to keep suspicion off him, but when the time was right, he would dispose of them both. He'd let Scott carry through with his plan so as to have the children, then he'd figure out what to do with the sheriff and deputy.

By nightfall, Everis and Shar sat two doors down from Scott Baker's house. The black jeep was partially hidden behind plastic trash bins. Everis removed a cardboard cup from the tray in his lap and handed it to Shar. "Settle in for a long wait."

She took the cup. "Thanks. I think the mother was telling the truth about him taking off. If he really was trying to immerse himself into Bishop's cult, they would have butted heads if the parents weren't like-minded."

Everis checked to see that Mayfield and Pinson were in place. "Anything happening?"

"Nope," Pinson replied. "We're parked in the trees so the goons can't see us. The place is locked down tight. Reminds me of my grandmother's retirement home."

"Keep your eyes peeled and your head down." Everis hung up. He didn't trust Bishop as far as he could spit. The man might seem friendly, but inside rested a coiled snake ready to spring. He slouched down in his seat and did his best to get comfortable.

"We could pass the time by making out?" He wiggled his eyebrows.

"Stop." She ducked her head. "That would be the time Scott would show up. How would I explain to the news that we missed him because we were acting like a couple of teenagers?"

He shrugged. "Can't fault a guy for trying. It's been a long time since we were just man and woman, not sheriff and deputy."

"We will be that again."

He would guarantee it. After they brought down

Bishop and rescued the girls, he planned on having Shar change her name from Camenetti to Hayes. All he'd have to do was convince her to say yes. Shar wasn't one to give up her independence.

"There." Shar flung open her door and darted into the night.

Everis made a sound deep in his throat and took off after her. "Wait up. You can't go chasing someone in the dark alone."

"Veer right. I'm going left. Baker is behind the houses." Without waiting for him to agree, she disappeared.

He would wring her neck when they rejoined each other. Everis cut right, taking the alley behind the houses. A figure jumped a chain-link fence and shot across a lawn. Everis followed.

"Halt. Deputy."

Scott Baker, lit for just a moment by the illumination of a motion-sensored light, glanced wide-eyed over his shoulder. He hunched his shoulders and scaled another fence.

Everis was getting too old for this. All this did was make him angry.

"I will shoot you," he called after the fleeing boy.

"No, you might hit me." Shar rocketed from his right. "Don't let him get away."

"I'm trying not to."

Again, he and Shar veered away from each other, trying to box Baker between them. They emerged onto the street. The boy was nowhere to be seen.

Shar groaned. "What do you think he was coming home for?"

"Let's ask his mother." Everis headed toward the

Baker home. They were being lied to, and he planned on getting to the bottom of why.

He banged on the Baker front door and rang the doorbell until Mr. Baker, bleary-eyed and irritated, answered. "What?"

Everis pushed his way inside. "I'd like to speak to you and your wife regarding your son."

"Scott ain't been here in days."

"So your wife said, but we just chased your son through the alley." Everis swiped his forearm across his sweating forehead while Shar kept guard at the front door. "Is your wife here?"

"I'm here." Mrs. Baker stepped from the hallway. "Scott just needed some clean clothes. You can't fault a boy for that."

Mr. Baker frowned. "You didn't tell me you've been in contact."

She shrugged. "I didn't think you cared."

"Why did you lie to us, Mrs. Baker?" Everis fixed a stern stare on her face.

Her features hardened. "If my boy did take those girls, it was because of the greater good. We're preparing for the future."

Mr. Baker threw his hands up. "Don't tell me you fell for that nonsense."

"It's going to happen. It's not a matter of if, it's a matter of when." She lifted her chin. "I intend to do all I can to make sure that the world goes on with my son in it."

"Then I suggest you tell your son to turn himself in before he gets killed," Everis said. "That could have happened tonight."

Her face paled. "Please don't kill my boy. Our

young people are the future. He's only doing what he believes will help the world go on."

"He's breaking the law and kidnapping." Shar moved forward. "You're aiding and abetting." She pulled her handcuffs from her belt. "You have the right to remain silent—"

By the time she'd finished reading the woman her rights, Mrs. Baker was sobbing. "Tell Scott I love him."

"For crying out loud, Martha. I'll be there in a few minutes to bail you out." Mr. Baker cursed and shoved his bare feet into slippers. "I'm sorry, Sheriff, but my wife and son don't have the sense God gave a goose."

Everis would have to agree with him on that. He gripped Mrs. Baker by the arm and led her to the jeep.

Chapter Eighteen

Scott Baker stared at the sheriff's house from his vantage point in the oak tree at the edge of her property. Once she drove away, he planned to carry on with the reverend's orders. He might have to dispose of the sister. Something that gave him pause. He'd never killed anyone before.

He felt the gun in the pocket of his hoodie. He could do it for his future. Sacrifices had to be made, just as his mother had spent the night in jail. Once Scott's position was secure in the church, he'd bring his mother into the fold. She may not be able to bear children, but she would be a faithful teacher.

He froze as the sheriff stepped onto her porch. She turned and placed a kiss on her baby's forehead, patted the deputy's son, then strolled to her jeep as if she hadn't a care in the world. Of course, she didn't. The reverend didn't force her to stay in the community despite saying he would many times. Even the deputy was hit-or-miss at sleeping in his room. Things had to change, and Scott was the one to change them.

Once the sheriff was out of sight, Scott jumped to the ground. Keeping low, he made his way to the back of the house and set a steak next to the bottom porch step. He couldn't poison the dog—animals were innocent, but he had no problem with letting them sleep for a while.

Sooner or later, the dog would be let out. Then, the sister would wonder what was keeping the animal and come out to investigate. That's when Scott would make his move.

Finally the giant dog came outside. He sniffed the steak, then left it alone while he skirted the yard.

Scott frowned. What dog didn't like a T-bone? New plan.

When the dog squatted to do his business, Scott made a dash for the house. He could hear the heavy thuds of the dog's paws as he gave chase. Scott burst into the door, leaving a piece of his hoodie in the dog's mouth.

The sheriff's sister stared with wide-eyes, then lunged for a knife on the counter.

"No, ma'am." Scott aimed the gun at the woman and locked the door behind him.

The dog scratched and leaped at the door.

"Let's get the girl and little ones, all right?" He motioned with the gun. As he stepped into the hall behind the woman, the front door slammed. He cursed as Mira raced away.

"Didn't count on that, did you?" The sheriff's sister smirked.

"Plan C."

"What were plans A and B?"

"It doesn't matter. Get the babies. Make it fast or

I'll shoot you and get them myself."

"Your hand is shaking, son. I don't think you're cut out for a life of violent crime."

"Don't make me prove you wrong."

Shar set the cardboard carrier, which held coffee for the men waiting for her at the office, on the hood of her jeep and answered her phone. "Mira?"

"He has a gun! I ran out the front."

"Wait. Who has a gun?" Shar's knees threatened to buckle.

"Scott Baker. He's at the house with Candy, Brian, and Robby."

"Where are you?"

"Hiding in that clump of bushes at the end of the driveway."

"Stay there. I'm coming." Not bothering to grab the coffee, Shar slid into the driver's seat and called Everis. "Meet me at the house. Now. Scott Baker has Candy and the kids."

"On my way." Click.

Shar parked next to Mira's hiding spot and told her to get in the backseat of the jeep. "Lock the doors, but be ready to open them if you see one of us coming."

"Be careful." Mira did as instructed and stared out the window.

Shar crept through the trees toward the house. Goliath immediately came running. "Good boy." She moved closer, Goliath at her side.

The crunch of gravel behind her told her that Everis had arrived. Seconds later, he joined her and Goliath. "Do we know if the babies are still there?"

"Yes. Candy hasn't left yet. I don't think he'll hurt

them. It's my sister I'm worried about." She would serve no purpose to the young man or to Bishop. "I'll take the back."

"Be careful."

Shar nodded and jogged to the back of the house. She frowned at the steak left on the step, then tossed it into the nearby trash can. "Good boy, Goliath." She snuck onto the porch and plastered her back against the wall. Leaning slightly to the left, she peered in the window. The kitchen was empty.

Robby's cries drifted through the bedroom window upstairs. He quieted quickly. Candy must have led Scott to the second floor. Shar slowly opened the back kitchen door and slipped inside.

Moments later, Candy, the children, and Scott appeared in the doorway.

The front door banged open. Everis appeared, followed by the dog.

Goliath rushed toward Scott.

Scott swung his gun from Everis to the dog.

Shar aimed and pulled the trigger.

Scott spun, then fell. The gun clattered to the floor and slid out of his reach. He scurried toward it only to be stopped by a mastiff standing on his back.

"Get him off!"

"Down, Goliath." Shar snapped her fingers. "Candy, Mira is at the end of the drive in the jeep. Please take the boys and join her."

"Gladly." She squeezed past Everis and hurried outside.

Shar kicked Scott's gun further out of his reach. "Get up."

"I can't. You shot me."

"It's a flesh wound. Get to your feet." He was darn lucky she didn't shoot to kill. No one threatened her family. She grabbed his arm and yanked him up.

Everis grabbed the other arm and pulled it behind his back. Seconds later, Scott stood bleeding from his thigh with his hands in cuffs. "Let's go, buddy." He prodded the boy forward. "Have a seat on the steps while I get the car. Shar, can you handle him?"

Scott's eyes widened. "Can't you stay and send her for the car?"

"If the sheriff doesn't stay, then who controls the dog?" Everis flashed a grin and jogged to his car at the end of the drive.

"Can't I get an ambulance?" Scott peered up at Shar.

"I'm thinking about it."

"That's police brutality."

"No more brutal than kidnapping my family." She kept her gaze focused straight ahead. She knew Everis would call for an ambulance from his car. It wouldn't hurt Scott to worry a bit.

Fifteen minutes later, he was strapped to a gurney and put in the back of an ambulance. "We'll see you at the hospital." Shar smiled and closed the doors.

* * *

"That could have ended bad," Everis said as the ambulance drove away.

"But it didn't." She rushed to her jeep and opened the door, pulling Robby into her arms.

Brian ran to Everis. "Daddy."

"That was quite an adventure, wasn't it?" His son had seen too much violence in his short life. Everis needed to find a way to prevent him from experiencing anymore. He kissed his son and gave him a long hug, resting his cheek on the top of his head. "I love you, son."

"I love you too, daddy."

Everis set him on his feet and turned to Candy. "We've got to go."

"I can handle things here."

"Keep the spare gun with you at all times and the doors locked. Goliath can hold it until I get home." Shar handed Robby to Mira. "You did good, Mira."

The girl grinned. "Was Scott the one kidnapping the girls?"

"We believe so."

Her smile faded. "I hope you find them." She headed for the house.

"Let's go question Baker," Everis said, sliding into the passenger seat.

When they reached the hospital, they were informed the young man had been assigned to a private room and handcuffed to the bed. Everis expressed his thanks and went with Shar to Scott's room.

The boy glared at them from the bed. "I had to have stitches."

"Where are the girls?" Everis stood as close to the bed as he could get without joining Scott on it. Shar did the same on the other side. Maybe them looming over him would intimidate the boy into talking.

"I don't know."

"You're in enough trouble. You might as well tell us."

"I'm telling the truth. I don't know what happens to them after I drop them off."

"You're lying." Shar leaned close. "Oh, no, I'm so

close to falling and pressing on your wound."

"That's against the law." He glanced at Everis. "She can't threaten me like that."

"Like what?"

"Who did you hand the girls over to?" Everis glanced toward the door. The boy was right. They couldn't question him without legal counsel, but they were running out of time.

"The reverend." Scott grinned. "He's going to make me an elder, and I get Carol for my first wife."

"An elder at the age of eighteen? You really are special." No doubt Bishop planned on getting rid of the boy when he was no longer useful.

"I want my lawyer. Where's my dad?"

Mr. Baker stormed into the room and straight to his son's side. He glared down at the boy. "You deserve whatever happens to you. How could you kidnap those young women? You're no son of mine." He clenched his fists, then took a deep shuddering breath before relaxing his hands. "You'll spend a long time in jail, Scott. Your mother will be alone. I can't live with her knowing she knew what you were doing." He shook his head. "I can't believe this is happening. I didn't raise you like this."

Scott shrugged. "I'll miss you in the new world. It doesn't matter that I'll be going to jail. When things come close, I'll be freed."

Everis couldn't believe the level of brainwashing. Scott truly seemed to believe what he was saying. He motioned his head toward the door.

Shar nodded. "Mr. Baker, please let us know when Scott's lawyer arrives."

"He'll need a public attorney. I'll not fork over the

cash." Mr. Baker whirled and stormed from the room.

"It saddens me that my father can't see the light," Scott said.

"It saddens me that you can be so stupid as to believe that nonsense." Shar stepped into the hall. "I don't want any visitors," she told the nurse's station. "Not a single one. Not a pastor, a preacher, or a reverend. Not his father, not his mother. When the public defender arrives, text me his name before allowing entrance. We'll be assigning a guard at the door as soon as possible."

"Mayfield again?" Everis asked.

"Or Pinson. They can share this duty, and the agents can pick up the slack. I do not want anyone from The Church of Superior Essence saying another word to that boy."

* * *

The reverend watched as the sheriff and the deputy marched through the main gate. He stood rigid, hands clasped behind his back. "It's not even nightfall."

"We thought we'd get an early start." The sheriff stopped in front of him. "We've arrested Scott Baker for the abduction of several girls."

"That's wonderful to know that justice is being served."

Her eyes glittered. "I won't stop until they are returned to their families."

He forced a smile. "That's what I admire about you. Your tenacity. That's a trait we'll need in the new world."

She opened her mouth to say something, but stopped when Deputy Hayes put a hand on her arm. "We're tired, Reverend. Would it be a problem if we turned in early?"

"Not at all." He stepped aside and watched as they split off and went to their respective dormitories.

They might suspect his involvement in the abductions, but they would have a heck of a time proving his guilt. It would be the word of four young women against his people. Majority would rule. Scott had brought the girls in on his own accord and hidden them in the underground bunker.

An easy story to tell. He'd convince the community of the importance of sticking to the story. They all knew what happened when someone went against his authority.

Chapter Nineteen

After an afternoon nap and then a supper ruined by Bishop droning on and on about community sticking together, Shar retired early to her room. She swallowed the capsule Agent Mills had given her. At two a.m. she met Everis by the outhouses.

"If you don't hold someone above ground, where do you put them?"

Shar smiled. "Underground. We just need to find the entrance."

"Let me show you, Sheriff." Bishop and his guards stepped from the shadows. "You too, Deputy. I no longer believe you are serious about joining my church. Perhaps you could do with some convincing." He stepped back while the guards held guns on Everis and her.

Shar squared her shoulders, refusing to be cowed, and went where the guards told her. They stopped next to the chapel. One of them pushed on a stake next to the steps. The steps fell, turning into the entrance to an underground bunker.

"Where better to store my precious possessions than under the church?" Bishop led the way down a concrete hallway.

Doors branched off each side. One of them held the girls, she knew it.

"Give me your phone." Bishop held out his hand.

Shar handed it over, fighting the urge to bash him in the head with it. One of the guards opened a door and pushed her inside. The other did the same to Everis. Then everything turned dark.

Shar fumbled around, sliding her hands along the wall until she found a narrow cot. She sat on the edge and prepared to wait for whatever Bishop had in store for her. Torture? Death? She leaned back against the wall.

Suddenly, Bishop's voice blared from a hidden speaker as he recited the same phrase his people repeated every night after supper.

Shar groaned. So, torture it was. She spread out on the cot and did her best to let her mind dwell on pleasant things like Robby's laugh or Goliath's big brown eyes or the way she felt when Everis gazed at her, then tenderly kissed her. While she'd do everything in her power not to die in Bishop's hidden bunker, her hope was fading.

She didn't know how long the recitation went on before it stopped, but stop it did. Just when the ringing in her ears subsided, it started again. Shar covered her ears with her hands and rolled to her side.

When she thought she'd go crazy, the door opened and the noise ceased. The light flickered to life, temporarily blinding her. The two guards entered the room, grabbed her by the arms, and dragged her into the hall. They pulled her along with them, down another corridor, up a flight of stairs, and into Bishop's office.

"You're looking a bit more submissive," he said as Shar was forcibly held in place in front of him.

"Not really." She forced a grin. Her ears still rang from the recording of his voice.

"More of the same then." He steepled his fingers. "Eventually you'll cave, my dear Sheriff. If this method doesn't work, I have others that may."

"Where's Deputy Hayes?"

"Enduring the same treatment, I assure you."

"Are you hurting him?"

"Not yet." His smile widened. "What the two of you endure is completely up to you." He waved a hand at one of the guards.

Before Shar could register what was happening, the man delivered a powerful punch to her gut. She gasped and bent over. If not for the grip of the other man, she would have fallen to her knees.

"That is just a taste of what is coming." Bishop chuckled. "I no longer want people like you and the deputy, but I do want my followers to know what happens to people who pretend an interest only to use it against me."

She blinked back the tears and forced herself to stand upright. "I can take whatever you dish out."

"Then this will be fun. Take her to the next room."

Fear ripped through Shar. She struggled to keep her mask in place. She couldn't let Bishop know the effect his words had on her.

She was tied to a straight-back metal chair. A few minutes later, Everis was pushed into the room. With his hands tied behind his back, he wasn't able to stay on his feet and fell hard to the cement floor.

His eyes flashed at the sight of her. "What are you doing?"

Bishop paced between them. "We'll be making a recording. Something to show as a warning of what happens when someone disobeys me."

"There's nothing to disobey," Shar said. "We never joined you."

"Others do not know that. Then, you'll be killed and disposed of. I'll comfort your families in their grief and offer them a home."

"Don't touch my son," Everis used the wall to get to his feet.

How long Shar wondered until her deputies realized she and Everis had disappeared? That they weren't just spending their night at the compound? How soon until they called the agents? Knowing full well it might be too late, she resigned herself to endure the time she had left.

Her head was yanked back and a cotton cloth placed over her face. Water hit her with the force of a faucet on full blast. She fought and jerked, trying to breathe. From across the room she heard Everis yell for them to leave her alone.

When the water stopped, she gulped for air, swallowing water still dripping from the rag. Before she fully recovered, the process was repeated. A strong desire to kill Bishop rose in her chest. Hatred would keep her going until waterboarding took her last breath.

Everis couldn't tear his gaze away from Shar thrashing as water was poured over her face. He strained against the zip ties on his wrists until the blood flowed. "Stop it! Take me instead."

"Your turn is coming, Mr. Hayes." Bishop sat in a corner of the room and crossed his ankles. "It's always ladies first in your world, isn't it?"

Shar went limp and Everis's heart stopped until he heard her drag in a ragged, watery breath. One of the guards pulled her from the chair and tossed her in the corner as if she were nothing more than a rag doll. Her head hit the wall and she lay still.

Fire burned through Everis. No matter what it took, he would make sure Bishop paid.

The guards dragged him to the chair and proceeded with the water torture. Over and over they took him to the point of suffocation or drowning only to give him a moment to recover before starting it all again.

Then, when Bishop determined he'd had enough he was dragged back to his room and the recording played. Shar had been taken away some time during his torture, and not knowing whether she was alive or dead ate at him.

He sat on the edge of his cot, too weak to lift his head, and fought to get his breathing under control. He'd been in bad straits before. The agents would come and rescue them. Then he'd make Bishop pay.

Plotting his revenge against Bishop kept him from going insane as the hours passed and the recording was shut off, then turned on, and so on. Once during the silence, he thought he'd heard someone scream and strained his ears to determine if it was Shar. All he needed to keep going was to know she was alive.

* * *

Shar woke to a pounding head, aggravated by the loud recording. She put a hand to her forehead and brought it away sticky with blood. Surprised she still lived, she sat up and hung her legs over the cot. Why hadn't Bishop continued the torture until he succeeded in killing her? How much longer until it was over?

Someone screamed and Shar jerked. A female scream. She stumbled through the dark to the door and pounded on it. "Who's there? This is Sheriff Camenetti. I'm here." She didn't know if they could hear her or not, but maybe she could give that person a sliver of hope.

The recording stopped, and she called out her name again.

"Thank God. Shar!" Everis's voice came from across the hall.

Shar leaned her forehead against the door and cried tears of relief. The recording started again, but it didn't seem as bad now that she knew Everis was only a room away.

The recording stopped.

"I'm Lauren Helms. I have Megan, Carol, and Ashley with me. Please tell me help is coming. Please." Her voice broke.

"Help is coming," Shar called out. Then, in a whisper to herself, she said, "help is coming."

She didn't know how she did it, but she fell asleep despite Bishop's noise. When she woke, all was quiet. Her cell had grown hot, and perspiration ran down her back, drenching the cotton gown she wore.

What day was it? Sunday? If so, Bishop and his people would be in town attending church.

Shar made her way to the door and tried the handle. Locked. She hadn't really expected it to open, but had to try. "Everis?"

"I'm here, sweetheart. Are you all right?"

"I'm hot and have a headache, but still alive."

"Keep hanging on. Mayfield and Pinson have to have noticed we're missing by now. They'll use the trackers."

Thank goodness hers hadn't been propelled from her stomach with the punch the day before. "I sure hope it's before Bishop returns." She couldn't survive the water torture again.

When Bishop returned, the guards once again hauled Shar and Everis into the cement room. This time, Bishop's son was there.

His eyes widened at the sight of Shar. "What's going on? Father, what have you done?"

"These two have done nothing but toy with us, Junior. They must pay, then die. We cannot have their rebellious kind in our new world."

"You cannot kill law enforcement, or you'll never make it to the world you're preparing for. You'll go to jail."

"If so, god will set me free before the end."

"Listen to him, Donald. Your father is crazy." Shar struggled against the guards holding her. "You can see that now. He's going to drag you down with him. I am going to kill you both."

"You can try, but ethics will prevent you from doing so. No, you'll try to lock us up." Donald glanced from Shar to his father and back again. "I'm to take over when he's gone. If he goes to jail, I'm the leader sooner."

Shar could tell the man had made up his mind. "Then you are no better than he is."

"Perhaps not." He focused back on her, running his

thumb down her cheek. "You are so lovely and smart. It's a pity. Father, I won't have any part in her killing." He turned and exited the room, leaving the door open.

"Not stopping him is just as bad as if you were the one doing the killing!"

Shouts sounded, then the pounding of feet.

Chapter Twenty

Donald pointed the way for the arriving agents, then followed protocol in fleeing the community. His wives knew what to do. Father would dart into a tunnel behind a hidden panel. Smiling, Donald ducked into another hidden passageway.

When he emerged at the exit hidden away in the woods, his father soon followed. "How did those agents know the sheriff and deputy were here?" He glowered.

Donald stared for a moment and shook his head. Sometimes he worried about his father's mental state. Perhaps he was growing senile in his sixties. "Don't worry about that now. They'll be coming for us."

Like ants, the residents of the community scurried through the woods on their way to the buses waiting for such a time as this. Donald grabbed his father's arm. "Come on."

"Everything I worked for is gone."

"No, it isn't. Everything you worked for is getting on those buses."

Shouts from the compound spurred him on. He

leaped onto the first bus and slid into the driver's seat.

They could start again. This time, maybe somewhere farther from a town. Somewhere they could live in peace the way his father dreamed.

* * *

"Give me a gun." Shar jumped up once her hands were free.

Agent Rollins handled her a 9-millimeter handgun. "Are you well enough to pursue the suspect?"

"I'm going to shoot him. The missing girls are down that hallway." Gripping the weapon, she pointed, then darted from the underground bunker.

Women and children fled for the woods. A few young girls raced for the gate. Good. At least some of the people here had some sense.

Shar switched direction and chased after the fleeing crowd. When she entered the forest, the residents split up and filtered away. The roar of a large engine drew Shar in that direction.

She stepped into a clearing as several beaten-up school buses sped around the corner. She dropped to her knees. They'd gotten away.

"Come on, darling." Everis helped her to her feet and pulled her into his arms. "We'll get them. Right now, I want you checked out by a doctor."

"No." She tried to pull away. "We have to go after them."

"They aren't going far. Bishop is too crazy to leave this as it is." He took her hand and tugged her after him. "We've plenty of people willing to testify against him."

With one last glance over her shoulder, she let him lead her to a waiting ambulance. The abducted girls leaned against a police car. Thank God they hadn't been harmed. A bit on the skinny side, but alive and breathing.

Everis helped Shar into the ambulance and climbed in behind her. "The paramedics just want to make sure we don't have any lasting effects from the waterboarding."

Her lungs felt heavy, but they still worked. All she wanted was to be left to pursue the Bishop and his men and see that they spent the rest of their worthless lives behind bars. She submitted quietly to a cursory examination, then climbed from the ambulance. "I need a uniform. I can't keep wearing this thin, filthy nightgown." She also needed a shower and a big meal, a hug from Robby, and a relaxing evening cuddling with Everis.

Would she ever be able to have a normal life? With a husband and family? She exhaled deeply through her nose. Someday, maybe. Her gaze rested on Everis. She might even consider not running for sheriff again if it meant spending the rest of her life with him. They did make a good team though. She might consider stepping down to the role of deputy.

"Let's go get fed and cleaned up," she said, "then figure out our next move. Have pizza delivered to the office."

"You got it." Everis made the call for pizza as they headed to where Mayfield and Pinson waited.

"Thank you for alerting the agents to our disappearance." Shar stopped in front of them. "What took so long?"

Pinson leaned against her jeep. "You said you were headed here to snoop. We thought that's what you were doing. But when almost two days passed—"

"Two days?" That was all. Two of the longest days of her life.

"Maybe you should grab a few hours of rest before working," Mayfield suggested. "No offense, but you look like a pile of sheep dung."

Shar glared at him and climbed into the driver's seat of her jeep. "Get out of my way. Meet us at the office in half an hour."

She drove straight home, saddened to learn that the children were at day care. She glanced at the wall clock. One p.m.? She'd lost more time than she'd thought. While Everis drove home to change, she took a fast shower, donned a clean uniform, and tied her hair back into a ponytail.

Too much had happened in that house. It might be her childhood home, but the last year had brought turmoil and danger within its walls. She glanced around the room. Could she sell and leave or would it be more feasible to install a security system inside the house and out.

Goliath stared up at her, then nudged her with his head.

"I know, buddy. I've been gone a lot. I promise to spend some time at home once those men are behind bars." She rubbed behind his ears and headed to her jeep.

Everis had beat her there, probably taking a shower in the employee restroom. He also always had a clean uniform at the office, something Shar sometimes forgot to replace.

"I am so happy to see you." Amber tottered forward and wrapped her arms around Shar's neck. "Improper or not, I'm giving you a big hug. We were all so worried."

Shar untangled herself. "I'm fine. Everis ordered pizza. Will you make sure it's brought back as soon as it arrives." Her stomach growled in response.

Amber giggled. "I'll bring it right away."

Shar returned her smile and entered the conference room where her three deputies waited. Her gaze lit on Everis for a moment, before turning to the case board. "Well, we know who our perps are now. We just have to find them."

"I say we set a trap," Pinson said. "The man expressed interest in me joining him. Maybe I can pretend to resign from the department and let it be known I want to."

"That might work," Mayfield said.

Shar shook her head. "Bishop will be suspicious of any one of us from now on."

"An undercover agent?"

"No, he wants me and Everis. It's personal now. We need to find a way to draw him out."

"We need to challenge him," Everis said.

Shar snapped her fingers. "The girls who willingly left the community when the agents arrived…are any of them pregnant?"

Everis grinned. "I see where you're going with this. Even if they aren't, we can say one or two of them are, if they were married to any the men. Children are the most important thing to keeping Bishop's dream growing."

Everis, with Shar at his side, sat across from five young women who had fled the compound. Not the four abducted girls—these were ones who had been there for a while. Not one of them was over the age of eighteen. They were frightened and scared, darting glances between him and Shar.

"Would you ladies like a soda?"

They glanced at each other.

"You've never had one? We'll have to remedy that." He called for Amber to bring five sodas in.

The girls' eyes widened when Amber, wearing a tight red skirt and low-cut white blouse with a red bra peeking out, entered with a tray. "I brought doughnuts too. Enjoy." She set the tray in the center of the table and sashayed out of the conference room.

The girls were hesitant at first, but after one sip of their drink and one taste of a sweet doughnut, they were hooked. Everis felt a little guilty about introducing them to sugar. When they'd finished, Shar folded her hands on the table.

"We have a proposition for you girls. We're hoping you can help us bring Bishop's so-called church to an end."

"How?" One of them wiped her mouth on her sleeve.

"Were any of you married to one of the men?"

A pretty blond girl around the age of sixteen raised her hand. "I was married to Donald Junior."

"I was married to the reverend." The oldest of the five squared her shoulders. "We got wed three years ago."

"Any children?"

"Two, and a third on the way. I really hope you can get my babies back. I don't want them to turn out like him."

Everis grinned. They'd hit pay dirt. "We would like

to spread the word around that you're expecting and want the reverend to come and save you from the unbelievers. Will you do that for us? Both of you? We'll say you other three have backslid and like the outside world better. Will they believe us?"

She nodded. "They'll do anything for the babies."

That's what Everis was counting on. "We'll need you to appear on camera."

"What's that?"

He glanced at Shar.

"On television," Shar said. "A reporter will ask you questions, and everyone in the state will see you."

"The reverend doesn't have one of those."

"Maybe not," Everis said, "but he's always heard about our press conferences before. Word will reach him."

"I don't want to go back." Tears filled her eyes.

Shar reached across the table and placed her hand over the girl's. "You won't. You'll be on the news, then taken somewhere safe. We will not let him get you back."

Everis prayed they could keep to their word. Bishop seemed to have friends everywhere. While the girls enjoyed the rest of their introduction to modern food, he pulled Shar into the hall. "Where can we put five girls? They will want to stay together and separating them would be cruel."

"We can't use Candy, not and have her watch the children. I won't put them in danger by having them around these girls." Shar sighed. "What about a hotel with posted guards? The agents could stay with them, freeing Mayfield and Pinson to keep watching Scott—"

"He's been transferred to a federal prison."

"Then that leaves them free to help us. I would like a woman with the girls though."

"I'll make a call. I'm sure we can get someone sent down. I'll see what I can do while you babysit." He flashed a grin, then opened the conference room door. "We need to stash these five somewhere. Scott's four victims will be in soon to give their reports." Everis enjoyed working in the small sheriff's office, but sometimes the lack of space was a hindrance.

He closed the door behind Shar and went to make a few phone calls. Ten minutes later, he had the promise of a female agent being sent to take custody of the girls. They would be taken to an undisclosed location and brought back for the press conference.

"Deputy Hayes." Amber clip-clopped on impossibly high heels in his direction. "We have several more of those people wanting protection."

"Bishop's people?"

She nodded. "Women and children, mostly. A couple of men. They said something about missing the bus."

Everis raised his eyebrows. They didn't get away, so they decided to turn traitor. "I'll get to them as soon as I can. Have the four previously missing girls arrived?"

"I put them and their parents in the interrogation room. It's a bit crowded."

"I'll do the interviews in Shar's office. Keep everyone where they are for now." He started to leave, then stopped. "Find somewhere for those people to stay until they figure out the next step in their lives. A safe house or something."

"I know of a place for the women and children, but

not the men." She held up a finger. "The women's shelter will know of a place for them." She hurried away.

Everis was again surprised at how Shar had taken a prostitute off the street and turned her into an invaluable part of local law enforcement. He took a deep breath and headed for the interrogation room. He peered through the mirrored window and cringed.

Four agitated sets of parents and four frightened girls huddled around the stainless-steel table. As unpleasant as it might be, the job needed doing. He took a deep breath and opened the door.

Chapter Twenty-One

Everis sat across the kitchen table from Shar the next morning and nursed his second cup of coffee. Shar knew they should be out of the house and at work, but something ate at him and there was nothing to do but wait until he brought himself to talk.

He glanced up. "Megan Tims is pregnant."

"Bishop." Shar forced the word out.

"She said no, but she won't say who. We'll have to send her away with the other girls." He let go of his cup and sat back in his chair.

"If the baby doesn't belong to him or his son, she should be safe enough."

He shook his head. "Bishop said he'd kill her if she got rid of the baby, and she definitely doesn't want to keep it. Neither do her parents. The girl has a future, they say."

"So, they're scared." Shar closed her eyes and took a deep breath. It wasn't the unborn child's fault that its mother had made a mistake. Neither was it Shar's place to tell the girl and her family what to do. "Okay, we'll send her away too." So many people in the world wanted a child and couldn't have one, and here was a teenage girl willing to throw hers away.

She glanced at Robby smashing bananas on the tray of his high chair. Thank God, Mira had chosen to let him be born.

"None of the other girls knew anything other than the fact that the Bishops planned on marrying them into the community. They weren't mistreated other than not getting enough to eat and having to listen to his recording over and over. They'll receive counseling and move on." Everis sighed. "Hopefully, today's press conference will bring this maniac out into the open, and we can close down this nightmare."

"Without anyone getting hurt. Let's go." She cleaned up Robby while Everis prepared his son for the day, then loaded the children in the car and set off for the day care.

Once the children were dropped off, they then headed for the sheriff's office where reporters had already started to gather. "They really are like sharks circling at the scent of blood." She drove around back and parked before making a dash for the building.

Amber glanced up from her keyboard. "That out there is ridiculous."

Shar agreed. Smiling, she headed for her office to check messages and prepare. It wasn't long before a commotion rose outside, alerting her to the fact the refugees from The Church of Superior Essence had arrived. "Someone, rescue them from the shark pool, please," Shar yelled.

Mayfield and Pinson both thundered past her office, followed by the two agents mere seconds later. Good.

The four of them should be able to escort the girls safely into the building.

Shar followed and waited in the lobby as the very frightened young ladies were rushed inside. "You'll be all right," she said. "These gentlemen, along with Deputy Hayes, will be outside guarding us the entire time we're on camera. Sarah, did you memorize your script?"

"Yes, but can I have it with me to read from? I'm afraid I'll forget what I'm supposed to say."

"Of course you can. I'll be next to you the entire time."

Much too soon, Shar stood in front of the podium, surrounded by nervous girls and stoic-faced law enforcement. In front of her, eager reporters and photographers crowded close. She held up her hands and waited until the crowd quieted. "Please, no questions until I say we're ready, and step back. These young ladies are nervous enough without you breathing on them."

She turned and motioned Abigail forward. "This is Sarah. She speaks for herself and Rachel." She took a step to the side, so the young girl could approach the podium.

Sarah's hands shook so hard they rattled the paper. Still, bravery won and she lifted her mouth to the microphone. "My name is Sarah." She shook her head. "No, it isn't. I'm Stephanie Evans. I'm seventeen-years-old, and I've been with the church since I ran away from home three years ago. I've been raped and beaten at the hands of Donald Bishop, Sr. and I carry his child. Leah is pregnant with the reverend's son's baby. We are hereby denouncing all ties with the church and are seeking our birth families. Thank you." She stepped back, practically hiding behind Everis.

"You did very well," Shar said softly, putting a hand on the girl's shoulder. "Very well."

"Does that mean I can have a soda?" Hope sprang into her eyes.

Shar's heart ripped. "You can have as many as you want." She took her spot behind the empty podium. "I will take your questions now."

The reporters all talked at once.

Pinson stepped forward and let out a shrill whistle. "Manners, people, or we're done here."

Shar chuckled. The man's uncouthness once bothered her. Now, she found it often comical, more often needed. The crowd quieted.

"Thank you, Deputy Pinson. You first, sir." She pointed to a man in the front.

"Do you know where Reverend Bishop has gone?"

"If we knew that, we'd have him and his men in custody. Next?"

A woman raised her hand. "What will become of the unborn babies?"

Shar glanced at Stephanie who shouted, "I'm keeping my baby."

"What happens to these girls now?" Someone shouted.

"They'll be taken somewhere safe until their families can be located."

"Your place?"

Shar gave a thin-lipped smile. "Next question." Hopefully, that would put enough information into Bishop's head to bring him to her.

"What about the girls that were abducted? Were

they sexually molested? Abused?"

"They say they weren't. It appears they were held in an underground bunker until mates could be found for them. No more questions." Shar turned and ushered the girls back into the building while reporters continued to fire questions.

* * *

Bishop cursed and threw a shoe at the hotel television. His blood ran in the babies those two girls carried. He had to get them back.

While they were nice and cozy at the sheriff's house, being reintroduced into an immoral world, he and his son languished in a rathole of a motel on a nearly deserted highway. His other men hid in tents in the woods.

Oh, the sheriff was going to pay. He'd known she was trouble from the moment he looked into her ice-blue eyes. A woman with hair like a raven had to be evil. She'd lured Deputy Hayes into her clutches with coy glances. Some men were too weak to resist her type. He wasn't, but he'd almost lost Junior to her grip.

His son entered the room with a bag of fast food. He glanced at the television. "I heard it on the radio. I never thought Leah would get pregnant."

"Your wife's name is Rachel. All your wives are Rachel."

Junior sighed. "We should change that rule. It's confusing." He handed his father a burger and fries. "Enjoy food from the modern world while you can."

"Yes, the world is fast approaching its end." He unwrapped the burger, the aroma tantalizing him with the lure of obesity.

"Maybe not in the way you think."

He jerked his attention back to Junior. "What do you mean?"

Junior shrugged. "I don't think we're going to make it out of this unscathed. At the very least, we'll be sent to prison. We'll be tried by the world's laws, not ours."

"We will prevail, son. Truth always wins." The reverend bit into his burger while his mind formulated a way to put his doomsday plan into effect.

* * *

"That ought to drag them out of the woodwork." Everis closed her office door behind him. "But I wish you hadn't alluded to the fact the girls might be staying with you. It's too dangerous."

"We need Bishop to come into town. I'll convince Candy to take the children on a vacation to Eureka Springs for a few days." She stacked some forms on her desk. "Did the girls get off okay?"

He nodded. "Pinson said he's getting used to being a babysitter."

She laughed. "No one will mess with those girls when he scowls in their direction."

"I wish you wouldn't be so frivolous with your safety."

She frowned. "I'm not. I take it very seriously, I just take the safety of this town more so." She tilted her head to the side. "Stop worrying, Everis. If it's my time, it's my time, and there is nothing you can do to stop that from happening."

"I thought I'd lost you in that torture room of Bishop's." He leaned against her desk and flipped her ponytail over her shoulder. "I don't want to watch you die. I don't want to have to tell your sister you aren't coming home."

"You won't." She placed a tender kiss on his lips. "I've endured a lot, Everis, and I can endure a lot more. This world isn't finished with me yet."

"Hmmm." He stood and moved for the door. "Don't do anything without me."

"I won't." She smiled.

With worry coating every inch of him, Everis left her office. With the girls gone and Bishop in hiding, he felt like an aluminum can blowing in the wind. He rattled around with nowhere in particular to go. The entire town seemed to be waiting, holding its breath for Bishop to strike.

When Ashley had been taken from her very own yard, the citizens of Highland Springs had finally heeded Shar's advice and stayed vigilant. Everis doubted things would return to normal until Bishop and his son were behind bars. So that meant there was very little to do until the snake struck.

He sat in the conference room and stared at the case board. The so-called church had been run out of the southern part of the state, somewhere outside Texarkana. Had they been in Texas before that?

Everis picked up the phone and placed a call. Ten minutes later, he had the location of their former property, still sitting unsold. He hurried to Shar's office. "I'm headed back to Bishop's land, then possibly heading south. Want to come?"

"Sure." She closed her laptop and followed. "What are you hoping to find?"

"Anything. The man I spoke with in Texarkana said no one was abducted, a few became converts, but most of the people in his area didn't want anything to do with Bishop and his crazy ideas. I'm hoping something might have been left behind to tell us his next plan."

Shar shuddered and turned away from the door leading to the cement room. That place had almost witnessed her last breath. Instead, she squatted in front of Bishop's desk and picked the lock on a drawer.

Inside rested several folders and another key. She flipped through the folders and found nothing. Clutching the key, she moved to a metal filing cabinet next to the door. She peered out to see Everis standing in front of the chair where she'd almost drowned. Either one of them could have died that day.

He shook his head and turned away, heading for a table at the far end. Shar had caught a glimpse of that table when they'd dragged her into the room. It held instruments of terror. Given the choice, she'd take the water.

The key fit the bottom drawer of the cabinet. A wooden box sat inside. She opened the box and pulled out a thick envelope. She pulled out the pages and started to read. Her heart plummeted to her feet. "Everis, you need to come here, please."

She sagged against the wall.

"What is it?" He hurried to her side.

"I know what Bishop is planning." She glanced up. "He's going to burn the town down. Look." She handed him the papers that spoke of the reverend's plan to burn up the towns of the people who turned away from the church. "Not only Highland Springs, but Texarkana as well."

Chapter Twenty-Two

"We have to get back to the office and warn the town citizens." Shar shoved the papers back in the envelope, then grabbed it and the box before racing for the jeep.

Once she was in the driver's seat, she stared at the compound. The buildings would most likely sit empty for years before a buyer was found...if the land went up for sale. No one would want to settle in a place where evil had once reigned.

"I'm ready." Everis slammed his door as Shar pressed the gas pedal.

Shar used Bluetooth to call Candy. "Get the kids and get out of town. Now."

"Wait, what?"

"Bishop is going to try and set the place on fire. I want all of you somewhere safe. Make sure Brian is with you." She cut Everis a sideways glance. He nodded.

"All right. We'll be out of town within thirty minutes. I'll let you know where we end up. Be careful, little sis." She hung up.

They parked in back of the station and ran inside. "Amber, go home." The girl lived far enough out of town that Shar hoped she would escape whatever hell was about to befall the town. "No questions, just go."

"Yes, ma'am." Amber grabbed her purse and ran amazingly fast for someone in stilettos.

Shar wished she could warn everyone to get out of town. Instead, she sent out a text advising those in town to go home and for businesses to close their doors until further notice. It was the best she could do.

"What is this?" Pinson asked, stepping into the hall and holding up his phone.

"War." Shar unlocked the gun cabinet and handed out rifles. "Only shoot to kill if someone's life is in danger. Bishop is coming to burn us out. I want the two of you to take up positions on top of buildings. Find the agents and have them do the same. Everis and I will monitor the streets. I'll text you a location if we spot someone. You do the same."

"Wow." Mayfield stared at the rifle in his hand. "I've never pointed one of these at anything but a deer." His gaze clashed with Shar's. "This is really happening? It's not a drill?"

"Not a drill." She grabbed Everis's hand. "Teamwork."

He squeezed back. "Teamwork." He pulled her close and gave her a deep kiss. "We'll be okay."

She nodded and blinked back tears. "Take your places, everyone," she said, stepping back. "I'm not sure whether Bishop will come today or another day, but we have to be ready."

Mayfield and Pinson looked at each other, then

turned as one and left the building. Shar took a deep breath. "Be careful, Everis."

"You heed your own words, will you?" He gave a lopsided grin that did nothing to dispel the worry in his eyes. "I know we haven't really discussed this, and maybe now isn't the time, but I love you, Sharlene Camenetti. When this is all over, will you marry me?"

Tears escaped and trickled down her cheeks. She swiped them away and gave an awkward laugh. "Not very sheriff-like to cry."

"But very woman-like. So?"

"I'll give you my answer when this is over." She couldn't tell him now. He needed to focus on the task at hand. Same as she did. "I do love you."

He pulled her close for another kiss, almost squeezing her breath from her lungs. Then he released her and rested his forehead against hers. "Let's go do this."

The reverend handed each of the ten men with him a backpack. "Burn this place to the ground and bring me the sheriff and her deputy dead or alive. If you find the wives, bring them to me, but only the pregnant ones. Kill the rest."

One of the men dropped his pack. "I'll have no part of killing. You want some fires set, that I'll do. But I won't take a life."

Bishop pulled a pistol from his belt and aimed at the man's head. "You will, or you'll lose yours. You pledged obedience."

"I joined a church, not an assassination circle."

Another man pulled him away. "Come on. Get your pack. I'll take care of this, Reverend Bishop."

"See that you do."

The idiot whispered that no one would know if they didn't pull the trigger. The reverend's finger twitched.

Junior pushed his hand down. "No, father. They're entitled to their opinion. They'll do what needs to be done."

"As will you. Right, son?" He clapped Junior on the shoulder. His boy would follow his commands as he'd been doing all these years. "Take care. I'll see you at the end."

The reverend climbed in a battered pickup he'd bought for a few hundred dollars from some drug addict and headed for the edge of Highland Springs. Dusk was the perfect time to set the sky aglow.

As he drove north, he thought of the church's next move. They didn't have an empty-headed reverend. Oh, no, they didn't. He'd bought other land in Missouri in addition to the land outside Highland Springs. He'd thought to use it as a second base, but it was large enough for his survivors. Construction on buildings was almost complete. Yes, they'd take care of the sneaky sheriff and her lying sidekick, then start fresh.

* * *

A plume of smoke drifted from the far side of town. Shar's phone began to vibrate with multiple voice mails. It had started.

She unhooked the radio at her belt. "Y'all see that?"

"Yeah," Pinson replied. "I saw a flash of light, then the smoke a few minutes later. Can't see anyone though. Mayfield?"

"Nope."

"Negative here," Everis said. "Where are you, sheriff?"

194

"Alley off Main."

"I'll meet you at the end." Everis hung up.

An explosion to the west shattered windows on Main Street, peppering Shar with glass. She ducked and covered her head with her arms. Once the threat of flying debris had subsided, she straightened and ran in the direction of the fire.

It wasn't until her right eye burned that she realized she'd been cut. She pressed the sleeve of her shirt against the wound and continued. Another explosion sounded to the east. Sirens wailed. There would be no way for the firemen to keep up when fires were starting up like campfires in a popular campsite. The whole business district of town could be gone by morning.

Everis caught up with her. "You're injured."

"Just a cut." She ran as close to the burning fast food place as she could. "There are cars here. That means there were people."

"No. Look." He motioned to where a handful of workers hid behind a truck.

"A man with a backpack came in," a young man wearing a manager badge said. "He told us to get out, then he threw down the pack and took off."

Shar prayed that meant those setting off the bombs weren't out to kill. If not, then why? What were they setting the fires for? To set an example? An explosion to the south set off car alarms. Hold on. She whirled.

"Everis, they're circling us. They're trying to trap us in." She whirled around to those by the truck. "Get out of town. Now."

"They knew we'd come out to make sure the residents were safe." He unclipped his radio. "Mayfield, Pinson, send any civilians you see out of town. Bishop is trying to trap us."

"Copy that." Pinson cursed before pressing the off button.

Shar kicked a nearby trash can. "This is nothing more than petty revenge. Why risk arrest by coming to town and committing arson?"

Everis shrugged. "The man is nuts. What can I say except we have to get out of here."

A fire truck raced past them. Two firemen hung off the back. "Help is coming," one shouted. "We can do this."

The firemen must be related to the optimistic Everis. Shar, on the other hand, was growing more pessimistic by the moment. "This way." She darted past the restaurant and into the alley behind the drugstore. Flames licked along the base of the buildings to her right. Minutes later, a team of volunteers converged with barrels of water.

"Absolutely not." She stood between them and the fire. "You have to leave. It isn't safe."

"This is our town too, sheriff," one of them said. "We did as you told us and got our families out of town, but we're staying to fight."

"They're right." Everis put an arm around her shoulders. "Let them do this. Bishop wants us. Let's keep moving away from people."

Donald Bishop, Junior stepped into their path, his hands held over his head. "Come with me if you want to live."

"Seriously?" Shar narrowed her eyes. "That's the corniest line from every thriller movie I've seen. You walked away to let us die back there."

"I didn't realize how far into the abyss my father

had gone. He won't stop until this entire town, and you with it, is gone." He started to lower his hands.

"Keep'em up." Shar aimed her weapon at his chest. "Why should we believe you? You want to take over when your father is gone. You'll say anything to achieve that goal."

"I'm not quite the zealot my father is." He glanced over his shoulder. "I've the scars on my back to prove it. Seriously, Sheriff, we have to go."

Another explosion, this one closer, knocked them off their feet. Shar lay on her back staring at the sky as she fought for her breath.

Everis offered a hand to help her up. "We have no choice but to let him go and continue on. Unless you want to run through this town with a prisoner in handcuffs."

"Not particularly." She grimaced and let him pull her up.

"I'd like to leave now if you don't mind." Donald motioned to where a group of men marched toward them. "My father won't be pleased to see me." He turned and darted between two buildings.

Shar couldn't help but think they should have kept him with them. She stared at the approaching horde. "Flee or fight?"

"Fight," Pinson said through the radio. "Bishop is in the center of the group. He has a bag over someone's head. We can start picking off the men surrounding him."

"I said no killing." Shar's skin prickled. They couldn't fight or flee. Not with a possible innocent being held. "We stand." She put her gun away and held up her hands.

"Well, hell." Everis did the same. "This cannot end well."

"I love you."

"Ditto, darlin'."

Chapter Twenty-Three

"The two people I wanted to see." Bishop grinned as his men removed Everis's and Shar's weapons.

"It can't be too big of a surprise," Shar said. "You planned it this way." She wanted to punch the grin right off his face. "Did you have to burn down my town? A simple phone call would have sufficed."

"Tsk tsk, Sheriff. I've only set fire to empty buildings or those rundown ones. I left the historical ones alone. After all, a town needs its history. Come with us, please." He waved his arm in a gallant gesture that did little to dispel the jab of a gun shoved in Shar's lower back. "We've one more fire to set while the brave firemen of Highland Springs put out the smaller ones."

"Small?" Everis frowned. "The skies are burning."

"Not really. We used a low-grade accelerant. I've no grudge against the town, only the two of you. I've brought you a visitor."

"Oh, goodie." Shar mumbled.

Bishop whipped the hood off the person walking

next to him to reveal a very angry Candy. "Ta da!"

Shar's heart almost stopped. "Where are the children?"

"Safe at day care and school," Candy said. "This no-good piece of trash had one of his men grab me when I left the day care."

"Let her go." Shar slipped her mask into place. She couldn't let the man know how much his having brought Candy scared her.

"I don't think so. Bringing your sister will insure you behave." Bishop led them inside the building he used for his in-town church.

"Have a seat, please. Deputy, you sit in the men's section, Sheriff, you and your sister sit on the other side."

"Keeping up appearance until the very end?" Everis sat. A muscle ticked in his jaw.

Bishop stood behind his podium. "There are a few things I want to say before we leave you to your fiery grave." His hands gripped the edges of the plain wooden structure.

Shar reached over and took her sister's hand as they sat. They'd find a way out. They couldn't give up hope.

Candy squeezed back. "Can you shoot him for me?"

Coughing to hide a laugh, Shar nodded. "I would love to."

One of Bishop's goons moved to stand at the end of their aisle. "No talking."

Bishop pounded the podium. "This is what I'm talking about. Disrespect for me, my church, and my people. I could have used folks like you in the coming new world, but not with the way you shrug off our faith as if it means nothing. Trial by fire, folks. If I were you,

I'd step into the flames and get it over with." He headed out a side door.

While three men held guns on Shar and the others, two more poured gasoline along the walls. Then they struck matches, tossed them down, and rushed after Bishop.

The walls ignited with a whoosh. Candy's eyes widened and her grip tightened. "There's no way out."

"We'll find a way." Everis joined them and grabbed Shar's hand. "Whatever happens, do not let go."

"I wouldn't think of it."

Already flames kissed the roof. The old building wouldn't take long to burn.

They tried the front door, only to find it bolted from the outside. The other doors were the same. They were going to die.

"There's no way out." Smoke burned her throat and caused tears to stream down her face.

"There is." Everis pointed to a window seven feet above the floor. "It's big enough, I think."

"How do we get up there?" A coughing fit overtook her.

"By piling up the benches. Hurry." Everis shoved one against the wall under the window, then broke out the glass with a pewter candleholder.

They had two piled and Candy was stretching for the window when a pair of hands reached in and grabbed her wrists. Donald's face appeared in the opening.

"I tried the doors, but they're nailed shut. I'd never get them opened in time. Come on." He yanked, dragging Candy through to safety. "Your turn, Sheriff."

She hesitated, not sure whether she should trust

him, but the heat on her back convinced her to try. She scrambled up and let him grip her hands. "Hurry, Donald. We have to get Everis out."

"Don't worry about me," Everis said. "I'm right behind you."

Something sharp grazed her ribcage as Donald pulled her through. "It'll take both of us to bring him up," she said.

"I've got a rope." Donald grinned and pointed to a length of rope looped on one end. "You can help me pull. Grab this, Deputy."

A few minutes later, a coughing Everis made it through. "We...have to...get clear. It's...going to fall." He struggled to his feet.

Shar propped her shoulder under his and the four of them lumbered to the safety of the parking lot. Sirens wailed in the distance. Help was coming.

Donald thrust a gun into Everis's hands. "My father will find out you're free and come after you. I can't shoot him."

Everis jerked. "You want me to kill your father?"

"If it means putting a stop to his madness, then yes."

"We'd rather throw him behind bars," Shar said. "Let's go. Candy, go to the day care and stay there until this is over. Bishop won't hurt the children."

"What about you?" She grabbed Shar in a fierce hug.

"We're going after him." Shar knew the man wouldn't stop until someone forced him to. "Don't worry. I'll be fine with Everis." He was probably the only one in the world, other than Candy, that Shar trusted with her life.

* • •

"Thank you." Everis held out his hand to Donald. When the man reached out to return the shake, Everis snapped a pair of handcuffs on him. "I appreciate what you did, but for your own safety, I'm turning you over to the federal agents."

Mills and Rollins hurried toward them. "We've got him." Mills took Donald by the elbow.

"Protection? More like arrest." Donald shook his head. "I expected it. I still couldn't let you die in that building."

"We appreciate that, and it will go easier on you during your trial." Everis clapped him on the shoulder. "I promise." He turned to Shar. "Let's finish this. Where would he go?"

"He's staying in that rundown motel off Larson Street, room seven," Donald said. "Try not to kill him, but he won't make it easy."

Agent Rollins handed Shar a pistol. "Stay safe. Mayfield and Pinson are scouring the streets for Bishop's men. We've taken six into custody so far."

"Good. Let's get every one of them, but right now, we need the deputies to meet us at the motel."

She ran alongside Everis to her jeep. "I know where that motel is. It's a seedy place that rents rooms by the hour." She peered over the hood of the car. "I will marry you, Everis. Today, tomorrow, or next week."

He grinned. "Then let's take care of Bishop and seal that with a kiss."

"I'll be waiting."

Fifteen minutes later, they sat across the road from the motel. A shadow moved on the other side of the curtains in the window of room seven. The manager had been alerted and advised to find a place of safety. Once Mayfield and Pinson arrived, they'd all move in.

"Any movement?" Pinson hunkered down next to Everis.

"Some, but we can't tell if it's Bishop or not." Everis glanced to where Mayfield took up a position next to Shar and handed her a Kevlar vest. "You two go around the back and try to gain entrance there. The sheriff and I will take the front. Try not to be seen. When I whistle, we break in."

"You got it." Pinson handed him a vest, then he and Mayfield skirted the parking lot.

Everis donned the vest, then glanced at Shar. "Ready?"

"More than."

Using cars as cover, they approached the motel. Everis stood with his back against the wall, Shar beside him, and strained his ears. "All I hear is the television."

"Then, let's hope Bishop is in there alone." She reached over and knocked. "Sheriff's department, open up."

Bishop cursed. The thudding of footsteps alerted Everis to the fact the man was trying to run out the back. He put his fingers to his lips and gave a shrill whistle.

Shouts came from the back of the building.

Everis stood back and kicked in the door.

Bishop turned away from the small window in the bathroom. "How did you survive?"

"Trial by fire, right?" Everis trained his gun on the man. "I guess the sheriff and I were found innocent. I doubt you'll be that lucky."

"I won't go to jail." He shoved a hand into his

pocket and pulled out a red capsule.

Shar shot him in the arm.

He dropped the capsule.

She stepped forward and ground it under her shoe as Everis tackled Bishop to the ground. He rolled the man over and pulled his arms behind him. "You have the right to remain silent. Yada yada." He got up and yanked Bishop to his feet.

"You're hurting me."

"I'd like to do a whole lot more than that." Everis shoved him toward the door as Mayfield and Pinson burst in. "Took y'all long enough."

"He was trying to squeeze his hefty self through that window," Pinson said, grinning. "Glad to see he's got a bullet in him."

"You're pretty bloodthirsty, you know that?" Shar holstered her weapon. "This means more paperwork for me."

He laughed and took over hauling Bishop outside.

Everis turned to Shar and held out his hand. "Can I kiss you now or should I wait until we're home?"

She stepped into his arms. "How about now and then?"

He wrapped his arms around her and lowered his face. "From now until the day I die." He pressed his lips against hers and pulled her as tight against him as was humanly possible. When they'd kissed until they were both breathless, he leaned his forehead against hers.

"I need a vacation with you. A long one."

"A honeymoon?"

"That sounds perfect."

The End

www.cynthiahickey.com

Cynthia Hickey is a multi-published and best-selling author of cozy mysteries and romantic suspense. She has taught writing at many conferences and small writing retreats. She and her husband run the publishing press, Winged Publications. They live in Arizona and Arkansas, becoming snowbirds with three dogs. They have ten grandchildren who keep them busy and tell everyone they know that "Nana is a writer."

Connect with me on FaceBook
        Twitter
        Amazon
        Sign up for my newsletter and receive a free short story
        www.cynthiahickey.com

        Follow me on Amazon

        Enjoy other books by Cynthia Hickey

        Shady Acres Mysteries
        Beware the Orchids, book 1
        Path to Nowhere
        Poison Foliage
        Poinsettia Madness
        Deadly Greenhouse Gases
        Vine Entrapment

        CLEAN BUT GRITTY

        Colors of Evil Series

        Shades of Crimson

CYNTHIA HICKEY

Coral Shadows

The Pretty Must Die Series

Ripped in Red, book 1
Pierced in Pink, book 2
Wounded in White, book 3
Worthy, The Complete Story

Lisa Paxton Mystery Series

Eenie Meenie Miny Mo
Jack Be Nimble
Hickory Dickory Dock

One Hour (A short story thriller)
Whisper Sweet Nothings (a sweet short romance)